RESCUE FROM
CAMP WILDWOOD

Timothy Peters

RESCUE FROM
CAMP WILDWOOD

TIMOTHY PETERS

PUBLISHING

Cover Design/Layout/Photo: Andrew Enos
Editing/Formatting: Erik V. Sahakian

All Scripture is taken from the New King James Version of the
Bible. Copyright © 1979, 1980, 1982 by Thomas Nelson, Inc.
Used by permission. All rights reserved.

Library of Congress Control Number: 2017948980

ISBN 978-0-9852857-4-6
First Printing: September 2017

FOR INFORMATION CONTACT:

Wildwood Ignited Publishing:
A Ministry of Wildwood Calvary Chapel
35145 Oak Glen Rd
Yucaipa, CA 92399
www.wildwoodcalvarychapel.com

Printed in the United States of America

TABLE OF CONTENTS

For my son, Jeremiah, his wife, Brittney, and their children, Benaiah, Guinevere, and Amos.

CHAPTER 1

Doug Powers started one of the engines on the Grumman's Goose as fifteen-year-old Joshua Powers sat in the pilot seat waiting to fly the airplane. His dad said it was just like flying his old Beech 18. Josh had never flown a seaplane before and this was going to be a thrill. The plane was built in the late 1930s and was still a good plane for Alaska.

"Joshua, start the next engine."

Josh primed the engine and hit the starter button. The engine turned over a few times and backfired. Smoke was coming out of the exhaust pipe.

"You have an engine fire, Son. Hit the starter again." Josh pushed the starter button again and the smoke stopped.

"These old radial engines catch fire inside. When you hit the starter it sucks the fire out. You don't have to use a fire extinguisher," said Doug. "Go ahead and try it again."

Josh nodded and pushed the starter button. The starter motor whined and the big propeller started to turn. It turned over three times and the engine roared to life.

The engines on the Goose were high above Josh's head and set out in front of the windshield. They were both loud and Josh was glad they had an intercom.

Both throttles and the propeller pitch control were above his head so he could reach them from the pilot or co-pilot's seat. There was a tunnel down under the dashboard that went to the nose of the airplane for the hatch so you could crawl out and throw a line to someone on shore.

Josh reached up, slowly pushed the throttles forward, and the plane started to move. He pushed the rudder pedal and turned the plane so it was headed straight down the channel.

"It is a beautiful day to have your first lesson in the Goose, Son. The water is as smooth as glass."

Josh was glad his dad was taking him over to Hoonah to get the airplane, Gabriel, an Airframe and Powerplant mechanic, said they could borrow. They had met Gabriel in the mountains when his dad was hurt during a fall after being chased by a bear.

The Mountain Goat was an airplane about the size of a PA-11 but had a bigger engine, wing flaps, and tundra tires. Josh was going to be the first to land on the runway they had cut out on their property.

When the family came to the island, Josh sat in the back of the Goose because he was so tired. He didn't get to fly the airplane that night, but today was his chance.

"The only things different about this airplane from the Beech-18 are the takeoff and landing," said Doug into his microphone.

"How's it different?"

"When you put the power in, the airplane feels like it is wallowing in the water. You have to wait for it to gain speed and when you push forward on the yoke it tilts up and gets up on the step."

"What's the step?"

"The step is when the plane gets up on top of the water," said Doug. "Let's give it a try. Put the power in."

Josh pushed the throttles forward and the engines started to roar. A spray of water covered the windshield. His dad reached up and turned on the windshield wiper.

The airplane slowly gained speed and he lifted the tail so the plane was up on the hull. Both wing pontoons were out of the water. After a longer takeoff run than Josh had expected, the Goose lifted gently into the air. Once in the air, it did fly like the Beech-18.

The landing was a little more difficult. Josh had to fly the plane down to the water, let it hit, and then cut the power. After another takeoff they flew over to Hoonah to get the little airplane. This time Josh had to lower the landing gear and land on the runway.

"You have to be careful never to land in the water with the landing gear down," said Doug. "The airplane will flip over if you do."

When they pulled up to the hangar, the Mountain Goat was sitting out in front.

"That airplane looks real good," said Doug. "Don't shut it down. I'll meet you back at the cabin."

Josh climbed out of the pilot seat and went to the door near the back of the plane. When he was on the ground he walked up to where his dad could see him and waved. Josh stood there and watched his dad take off.

The Mountain Goat looked like a great airplane. It was a bush pilot's dream and he would need it if he was going to land at the cabin. The runway was short and bumpy. He took off and headed up over the snowcapped mountains and forest toward the cabin.

A flash of light turned Josh's attention to the left. He saw an orange rectangle with a person dressed in red and then it was gone. He was in the middle of the wilderness area on Chichagof Island, Alaska. He circled around again to try to spot the reflection, but he couldn't find the place or the person. He was traveling over a very dense green forest and to see something in the middle of all these trees was difficult.

Josh tried to be scientific about it. He turned the airplane around and flew back in the opposite direction. He flew for five minutes then turned back 180 degrees. He realized he had not been paying attention to the trees. He knew where he was going so he wasn't really paying attention to his compass either.

The morning was beautiful with fluffy clouds, light rain, and sunshine breaking through the clouds. The forest and the island glowed in the sunshine like God had shined a floodlight right where he was flying.

Josh knew if the person had signaled him, they were in trouble. They probably heard the airplane and flashed a mirror when they saw it. But where was the person?

This was the first family vacation Josh could remember. The cabin had been given to him when Willa Snyder had died the year before. It was a beautiful cabin on the northwest end of Peril Strait. His father and mother had gone to the cabin two weeks before and his father had started to make a runway for his little plane. When Josh got out to the cabin, they finished the runway. His dad had called it the "In-n-Out Airport." Josh didn't know if he wanted to land on it.

But now, after spotting the bright signal from the person in red, he had to. He had to get his dad to go with him to look for the person.

Josh searched for an hour and could not find the man who signaled him. When he checked the fuel gauges on the inside of both wings, the fuel was getting dangerously low. He hoped he had enough gas to make it to their airport.

He flew back and forth, but never saw another sign. No orange rectangle, no mirror, and no person dressed in red. He turned his plane back to southeast and started for the cabin.

The weather was closing in. He had been so intent on finding the person, he had not kept an eye on the weather. The weather now looked like it was going to stop him. Stop him from finding the person and maybe even stop him from landing at the homemade airport. The clouds were slowly moving toward the ground and Josh had to hurry. He turned the plane back on course and started down over the tops of the trees. If he got down on the water he would probably have enough clear space to make it to the cabin.

"Father, help me to find this person."

He thought he might be able to reach the Coast Guard to look for the hiker, but he was not sure of that either. He put the power in and climbed back to the bottom of the clouds. He switched his radio to the emergency frequencies and pushed the button for his microphone on the stick.

"Coast Guard this is 6-6-Romeo. Do you read? Over." Josh didn't know if he should call it Piper Cub or not. He waited for a few seconds and tried again. "Coast Guard this is 6-6-Romeo. Do you read? Over." He repeated the same message ten times, but no one responded. He thought if there was an airliner out there somewhere they would relay the message, but no one seemed to be listening. The airliners were probably too far away to hear.

Josh reached up and switched the radio back to 122.9 the Unicom frequency. He knew his dad would be monitoring that one.

"In-n-Out Airport, this is 6-6-Romeo. Do you read? Over." After a few second his dad responded.

"6-6-Romeo this…" the handheld radio his father was using was cutting out. Josh was only able to hear a few words.

"Dad, you're breaking up. Say again!"

"6-6-Romeo…weather…where…" was all Josh heard.

He put the nose of the plane down and pulled back on the power. The plane started down through a ghostly landscape. The trees were beginning to look like dark, giant shadows through the fog. If he got down to the water, he could probably find his way. The clouds were going down as fast as he was. He started to worry this trip would end up like the trip to rescue his father from the drug dealers, but maybe he wouldn't be so lucky this time.

His heart started to race and he didn't want to crash again. How many crashes did one guy have in him? Would he survive if he did? He knew Alaska was hard on pilots and didn't want to be one of the fatality figures this year or any year. And it was a borrowed airplane.

"Father, You know I need Your help. Help me, please." No sooner had he said it then he broke out of the clouds two-hundred feet out of the water.

"Thank you, Lord!" was all Josh could say.

Josh recognized where he was immediately. There in front of him was Moser Island. He turned the airplane around and started back toward the end of Peril Strait. The little landing strip was to the left of the cabin. This scared him because the low clouds only gave him one chance to land. If he had to pull up and go around he wouldn't know where the mountains were. Josh pushed the button on his stick one more time.

"In-n-Out Airport, this is 6-6-Romeo. Do you read me? Over."

"6-6-Romeo. Go ahead," said his dad in a clear, unbroken voice.

"Dad! I'm coming in. The clouds are getting lower. How's the weather there?"

"The ceiling is about two-hundred feet. You're going to have to nail this landing. How far out are you?"

"I'm about ten or fifteen minutes out. Dad, I'm not sure I can do this."

"You can, Son. You're a good pilot. Slow the airplane down, use the flaps, and come on in low and slow. When you see the Goose, go right over the top of it."

"Okay, Dad."

Josh saw the channel was narrowing. The trees were becoming visible as he flew on. He searched the bay for the gray and aluminum color of the Grumman's Goose. It was a World War II seaplane his dad had borrowed from one of his old friends who flew with him in El Salvador, but now he was flying passengers in Alaska.

The Goose was in good flying order but it was ugly. Its navy blue paint was the only color it had, but it was coming off. One of the stars the military had painted on the upper wing was still partly visible. The belly, bottom of the wings, and both engines were painted white, but now even the white was wearing off.

Josh was glad his dad wanted to fly the Goose back to pick up this airplane. The flight had made his day. The landing was a little rough, but Josh felt like he could fly the airplane and was thankful he did.

The fog was getting lower as Josh approached what he thought was the end of the channel. He had to turn left and fly along the shoreline until he spotted the Goose. In the distance he could see the dark outline of the old airplane.

"Dad, I'm here." Josh's heart began to race.

"I see you, Son. You're off course and too high. Come left. That's good, now turn and go over the Goose."

Josh saw his dad out of the corner of his eye. Before he could say anything else his dad came back on the radio.

"Joshua, you're too high!"

Josh had forgotten to use the flaps. His PA-11 didn't have any so he stepped down on the left rudder and pulled the stick to the right to slip the airplane. The airplane sank down, but it wasn't enough.

"Joshua, go around now! Turn left, now! Turn left!"

Josh pulled the stick back to the left, pressed down harder on the rudder, and at the same time he pushed the throttle in with his left hand. The wing of the plane was almost straight down as he pulled back gently on the stick. The plane turned sharply out over the water. If he had turned the other way he would have hit the mountain, but there was nothing to hit the way he turned.

As the plane turned over the water, Josh leveled it out. The fog was getting lower and Josh was getting more nervous. Josh reached up and pulled down on the flap handle. The plane felt like it was lighter than air.

"Dad, I can't see the runway! Am I lined up?"

"Come right in over the Goose. Do you remember how to do a spot landing?"

"I think I do," Josh said into his microphone.

"I'm going to stand on the end of the runway. I want you to land right in front of me. You only have six-hundred feet of runway and then the mountain. Once you are down, you won't be able to go around. Joshua, we only have one more chance," said Doug softly.

"I know, Dad. This one will be good," said Josh, trying to build his confidence. "Father, help me land this thing so I can help the person out there," Josh prayed as he slowed the airplane down.

"You're still too high. Lower it down some, Son." The plane was down to fifty feet out of the water and flying slow. The Goose was coming up and Josh felt like he was going to hit it.

"You're doing good, Joshua."

When Josh got right over the Goose the stall warning horn sounded. Josh pushed a little more throttle in to speed the airplane up, but it didn't stop the horn. He pulled the power off and tried to land next to his dad, but he forced the plane down so it hit the ground and bounced. He let the back pressure off the stick and then brought the plane down in a normal flair.

The runway went uphill and the airplane slowed and rolled out into the fog. His rollout seemed like it lasted forever and when the plane finally stopped, Josh turned it around and started to taxi slowly back to his dad. His eye strained to see him. He didn't want to hit him with the prop.

Josh saw his dad standing off to the side of the runway motioning for him to turn. He turned the plane and looked at his dad who signaled for him to stop. Josh reached up to the dashboard and switched the airplane off as his dad walked up and opened the door.

"That wasn't a bad landing in the fog. I listened to your rollout and you didn't go too far. We'll have to check to see how far you went when the fog is gone."

"That was scary. I'm glad I'm on the ground. Dad, when I came over the top of the ridge someone flashed me with a mirror or something. There was someone down there dressed in red. I looked for him for about a half hour, but couldn't find him. Too many trees."

"I'll go up with you tomorrow and see if we can find him."

"I didn't want to leave them, but there was nothing I could do. It's why I got here so late. I looked for them so long I didn't notice the weather closing out."

"Joshua, we'll go up tomorrow and look for whoever it was. If we can't find them, when I go over to Hoonah, I'll call the Coast Guard. It was nice of Gabriel to loan you this airplane. It looks like you're an old bush pilot."

"It has a lot more power. I need to get used to it. The tires do make it look cool," said Josh. His dad walked over and picked up a bucket of dried cement and carried it over to the airplane. Josh picked up the rope and tied it to the ring on the strut and then to the ring in the cement. His dad got another bucket and Josh tied down the other wing.

Doug had nailed three pieces of split log together to make chocks he put on both tires. With the airplane secured, they turned and started for the cabin.

"Dad, I hope the person is okay. You know the bears up there are scary. He didn't have a fire going or anything."

"Father, we ask You to protect the person from the bears and give them a safe place to camp until we can get back there," his dad prayed.

"We'll go first thing in the morning and find them," Josh said.

"I hope we can go. You know the weather here."

When they got to the cabin his mother, Liz Powers, was standing on the front porch with her arms folded across her chest to warm herself from the cold, damp air.

"Joshua, I got worried about you. The clouds were closing in and the weather was getting worse. Then I saw your plane come in over the Goose and heard the engine speed up. What took you so long to get here?" said Liz.

"I spotted someone up in the hills, but I couldn't find them when I looked."

"Oh, I hope they're all right. You two come in by the fire and warm up. I'll get you something hot to drink," said his mother.

"I hope you like the changes we made to your cabin, Joshua," said Doug as he walked up the stairs to the front porch. "Hi, Honey, we're home now," he said to Liz as he leaned over and kissed her.

"I know, but I worry about Joshua on days like this. He doesn't have the experience you do," said Liz.

"He got some experience today. That's how you get experience. One little lesson at a time," said Doug as he patted Josh on the shoulder. "Isn't that right, Son?"

Josh nodded his head and walked into the cabin. It was still simple, but it had his mother's touch. There were new flowered curtains in each window and the kitchen had new curtains covering the cupboards. The dishes they used that morning were washed and drying on the counter next to the sink.

"Joshua, this is the main thing I changed in your cabin. I made this double bed out of some logs I found in the backyard under a tarp. We needed the Goose to bring the mattress out. And I built a bunkbed for you to sleep in on the other side of the room. We'll have to get another mattress for the top bunk," said his dad.

"Man, you work fast," said Josh. "I was so tired last night when we got here I hardly noticed the changes."

"This is the first time we have had a family vacation in a long time. Thank you for letting us use your cabin for R&R," said his mother. "That was nice of Willa Snyder to give you this gift." The whole cabin had a warm, homey feeling now that his parents were there. His mother had been a missionary long enough to figure out how to make any little old house seem like the Ritz-Carlton without much money.

Josh and his dad sat down on the couch in front of the fire and his mother brought three cups on a slab of wood to serve both men. When she came back from the kitchen she sat down between them on the couch. The cups were filled with steaming, hot clam chowder.

"This chowder is another little gift from Willa," said Liz.

CHAPTER 2

When Josh got up the next morning and looked out the window, he couldn't see past the front porch. The mist was drenching everything. He looked over at his mother and father's bed. His mother was wrapped up in the blankets.

"How'd you sleep, honey?" said Liz with a groggy voice.

"I slept great," said Josh. "It is so quiet here I could still be in bed."

"You're on vacation. You don't have to get up this early."

"I couldn't sleep anymore. We were going to find that person in the hills this morning, but we will have to wait. Where's Dad?"

"Oh, he said since it was foggy he was going fishing this morning."

Josh got dressed, put a rain coat over his clothes, and went out on the front porch. He couldn't tell where his father was fishing. He walked off the porch, stopped, and listened again. This time he heard a splash in the water. The sound came from out near the Goose.

He walked slowly out toward the sound. Something kept splashing and Josh wondered if it was his dad or a bear. When he got to the seaplane platform, he saw the outline of his dad reeling in a two-foot-long salmon.

"That's a nice fish, Dad," Josh said as he walked up to his father.

"It's the second one I've caught. I think I better stop fishing. We don't have a freezer out here. We'll have Mom cook these for dinner tonight."

Doug threw his lure out into the mist one more time. The reel buzzed and then there was a splash in the water. He turned the crank slowly on the reel.

"I'm sorry we can't go look for the guy you saw. This fog has us socked in. Maybe it will burn off in the afternoon," said Doug.

"I hope so. You remember how those bears were out there. We need to get him out of there." His dad nodded his head as he caught another fish.

Doug fought the fish for fifteen minutes. It was making a lot of noise, sloshing through the water. When he pulled it up where they could see, it was bigger than the two he had already caught.

"I think I better cut this one loose."

Josh waded out to the fish, reached down, put his hand in its gills, and pulled the head up out of the water. His dad handed him some needle-nose pliers and Josh took ahold of the hook. He twisted his wrist and the hook popped out. He dropped the fish back into the water. The fish turned and flapped its tail, splashing water all over Josh.

"Thank you, I needed that, Mr. Fish."

"That was a big fish. Too bad we had to let it go."

"Ah, there're other fish in the sea," Josh chuckled. "We'll take that one tomorrow."

Doug gathered up all of his fishing gear and Josh picked up the two big salmon.

"These fish are really big, aren't they, Dad?"

"Yeah, they're pretty good size. I was thinking, Joshua. When we go find this guy, we need to take a bullhorn."

"Where are we going to get a bullhorn?"

"Funny you should ask. There happens to be one in the Goose. Barry probably has it in there to hail shore or something."

"What can we do with a bullhorn?"

"When we find the guy, we'll open the side window and cut the power. Then we can talk to him through the bullhorn. We'll ask him yes or no questions and tell him to signal yes or no. We did it in El Salvador when we would find an Indian village out in the middle of the jungle. It works great."

"What if he needs food or something?"

"We'll make another trip out with a bucket and a long rope, and do a bucket drop. Nate Saint used it with the Acca Indians in Ecuador. He put the airplane in a tight right turn and let the bucket down on the rope. The tight turn made the bucket almost stand still. They could trade trinkets. If the person down there needs food, we can send something down."

"I sure hope the bears haven't bothered him," said Josh.

"Yeah, but you know how many bears we saw. He's probably seen at least one."

Doug stopped by a small outdoor table and cleaned the fish. He took the entrails out far from the cabin so they wouldn't have another problem with the bears. Josh carried the fish into the cabin and gave them to his mother.

"Those are beautiful fish," said Liz. "Did you catch these?"

"No, Dad did."

"Joshua, God has made a beautiful land up here. There's wildlife and dinner for the taking. It's hard to think this is under the control of the enemy, isn't it? You need to thank God for these surroundings every day."

After two more days of fog and rain, the sun broke through the clouds and seemed to melt them away. Josh woke up early with bright light streaming through the window. When he saw how clear the day was he walked over to his mom and dad's bed and shook his dad's shoulder.

"Dad, wake up. We can go today. Where is the megaphone?" said Josh in a whispered voice.

"It's in the bag right behind the pilot seat in the Goose." Doug got up and walked into the bathroom.

Josh went out the front door and was struck by his surroundings. The still morning air was filled with the sounds of birds and little splashes of fish jumping in the water. As he stood looking around at the beauty, he saw a deer grazing next to his airplane. Mist rose from the water like tiny ringlets of smoke.

"Father, thank You for this. Thank You for all You have created. Father, help us find this guy today. Keep him safe until we do. Amen."

Josh went to the Goose and opened the passenger door on the side and climbed in. When he got in, it rocked like a boat. He had to hold on to the backs of the seats as he walked to the cockpit to retrieve the bag. He put the strap of the megaphone around his neck and repeated the process to get out.

As Josh walked toward his airplane, the deer heard him coming and raised his head. It turned and then scampered away. When he was halfway there his mother came out on the porch.

"Joshua, have you eaten anything this morning?"

Josh shook his head, turned, and went into the cabin. His mother had hot oatmeal in a bowl on the table waiting for him. He bowed his head and silently prayed for breakfast and the beauty of his surroundings.

"Thanks, Mom. Where's Dad?"

"Your father is out back getting the gasoline for your airplane."

Josh tried to gulp his food down, but by the time he got outside his dad was climbing off the ladder with an empty five-gallon can and funnel.

"That should do it. Are you ready to go? If you are, I need to go tell your mother we are leaving. That's something I do every time I go. That's a good habit."

Josh and his dad walked back to the cabin and said goodbye. When they walked off the porch, Josh turned and waved to his mom one more time.

"Joshua, your mom is a good woman. I hope you find a wife as good as her in twenty or thirty years." His dad looked at him and smiled.

They each went to a wing, untied it, and removed the log chocks from the tires. Josh started to get in the back seat so his dad could fly from the front seat.

"Joshua, you get in the front seat. I'm going to talk you through this while you are taking off. You need to learn how to use the airport. You did a fine job landing the other day, but this might be a little trickier."

Josh nodded, got into the front seat, and his dad got into the back. He was ten feet above sea level so he set his altimeter to zero. He went through his checklist and started the plane. He turned the airplane and started to taxi up the hill to the other end of the runway. His dad looked out the window, trying to see how far he went on the landing. They were three-quarters of the way up the runway when Josh saw it.

"Dad, here's where I turned around the other day."

"That's not bad. You had plenty of room to roll out."

When they got to the end of the runway, Josh turned the plane around.

"Are you sure there is enough room to take off? This runway looks real short."

"This airplane should take off in one hundred feet. Pull the flap handle all the way down. This runway should be long enough."

Josh checked his instruments and had oil pressure. Then he checked the mags and started to run the engines up. He held the brakes as long as he could before he released them. The plane started to roll down the runway.

"Remember, this airplane will fly about fifty miles per hour. Try to wait as long as you can," Doug said in his microphone.

The airplane started off slow and then gained speed. Josh was listening to the plane to see when it was ready to fly. When he pushed the power all the way in the tail came up off the ground and picked up more speed. The airplane bounced as it traveled down the runway. It started to feel light, so he pulled back on the stick and checked the airspeed. It was indicating seventy miles per hour.

They cleared the Goose by one hundred feet. Josh steadily climbed over the island and turned the airplane around.

"That got off in one hundred and fifty feet. Not bad. Let's go back to where you saw this guy," said Doug.

Josh nodded and gave his dad the thumbs up. They flew about a half hour out into the forest.

"Man, the forest is really dense, isn't it?" said Doug.

"Yeah, that's why I couldn't find him."

"Do you remember what heading you were on when you saw him?"

"I think I was on a heading of 185 degrees."

"Let's go back to where you came over the ridge, turn to that heading, and fly your route again," said Doug.

"Good idea."

Josh turned the airplane toward the pass. When he got to the mountain pass, he turned the airplane around to a heading of 185 degrees. They flew along in silence looking intently out both sides of the airplane.

"Dad, I think we've gone too far."

"I wonder if they've moved?"

"I doubt it, Dad. They definitely flashed me with the mirror. And the big orange tarp on the ground was a signal."

"Yeah, you might be right."

"Dad, we're going to go back through the pass and try again."

"Roger that, Houston," said Doug.

Josh turned the plane around and flew back through the pass. After ten minutes, he turned the airplane and came to a heading of 185 degrees.

"Dad you watch out the left side and I'll watch out the right."

"Joshua, this forest is thick. If you're off a couple of degrees they will be hard to find."

"I know, but we have to keep looking."

"Let's go back and do the same thing again. Only this time, fly a heading of 187 degrees."

Josh turned his head and nodded to his dad. The airplane started a slow turn to the right. As they turned Josh raised his head and looked out the left side of the airplane for any other air traffic. Something bright orange caught his eye.

"Dad! There it is!"

"Where?"

"Look over to the left by the stream."

"I got it, Son."

"Keep your eyes on it until I can get the plane turned around."

Josh turned the airplane hard to the left. When it came over the site, the large orange tarp was folded like one of the rocks had come off the corner. And the red parka was lying on the ground, shredded and torn to bits. There was no one around the campsite.

Josh pulled the throttle back and then advanced it again. He did that several times. The noise from the engine should have brought someone out, but no one came.

"Joshua, I am going to try the bullhorn." Doug slid the window open on the left side of the cockpit. The cool morning air changed the temperature. Josh shuddered when the breeze got to him. Doug picked up the megaphone and held it out the window.

"Cut the power when I tap you on the shoulder."

"How long shall I leave it off?"

"I'll tap you on the shoulder again when you should put the power back in."

Josh circled around the orange tarp. He hoped the airplane noise would bring someone out.

"Okay Joshua, cut the power." Doug tapped Josh on the shoulder.

Josh pulled back on the throttle with his left hand. The silence was a welcome relief. When his dad had opened the window the roar of the engine increased. The plane was spiraling down toward the ground in silence.

"Hello down there. Is anyone there?" Doug said through the bullhorn. There was no movement or sound.

"Hello down there. Is anyone there?"

Josh started to tense up as the wing was getting too close to the trees. Just when he started to say something his dad reached up and tapped him on the shoulder.

"Put the power in and climb, and we will try again." Josh was glad his dad didn't give up.

Josh slid the throttle forward and the plane came back to life. He climbed to a safe altitude and waited for his dad to tap his shoulder again. Doug sat in the back staring down at the ground, looking for someone or something.

"Joshua, this doesn't look good."

"I know, Dad. But we have to try again."

Doug stuck the megaphone out the window again. This time he didn't say anything to Josh, he just tapped him on the shoulder.

"Hello! Is anyone down there?" Doug called again.

Nothing moved.

"Hello! Is anyone down there? Hello! Is… Joshua, look at the end of the giant log over to the right!"

Josh pushed the power in, turned, and looked at the log. There were two feet wiggling out of a big, dead log. They flew around in circles until the person was standing up.

"Dad! Dad, it's a girl!"

CHAPTER 3

"Cut the power, Son." Doug stuck the megaphone out the window again as Josh pulled the power off. "Are you okay?"

The girl seemed to yell something, but they could not make out what she said.

"If you want to say yes, hold both hands over your head. If the answer is no, then hold them out to your sides. Do you understand?"

The girl held both of her hands above her head.

"Praise God, she understands."

Josh put the power in and started to climb back to his altitude. When he got there, he cut the power again.

"Are you okay?" Doug asked again. The young girl put her hands straight over her head and then lowered them straight against her sides. Then she repeated the same signal again.

"This is one smart girl," said Doug.

"Are you hungry?" This time her hands shot up over her head.

"We'll have to bring her some food, Dad." Josh put the power in again and climbed back to altitude.

"Yeah Son, we'll do the bucket drop. You may have to practice that one." Josh cut the power.

"Have you seen a bear?" The little girl's hands went up over her head several times.

"Do you have a safe place to sleep?"

The girl put her hands up over her head and then pointed to the log.

"Do you have a fire?" This time the girl put her hands straight out from her sides.

"Are you alone?" The girl put her hands straight up.

Doug took the megaphone down from his mouth. "I wonder why she is out here all alone?" Before Josh could say anything he put the megaphone back up to his mouth.

"We will be back in about an hour with food and matches. Stay right there." The girl put her hands over her head.

Josh put the power in and widened his circle. The men started to look for a reference point they could use to find the girl again. The ground started to look familiar to Josh. He saw a cliff with a ledge down below and then a trail.

"Dad, that's where the bear got you. See the cliff and the trail down there?"

"That girl is about a half mile directly north of the cliff. Joshua, that's why God had us go through all of that stuff. We can follow the trail up to here and then turn and go north to the girl."

Josh wondered if God would allow a person to break their leg to teach them something. He thought of people in the Bible like Jacob who received a lifelong limp learning something from God, and Joseph who had endured false accusations and prison for twenty years. He remembered from a sermon that Joseph said, "Man had meant it for evil, but God meant it for good." His thoughts were interrupted by his dad.

"Let's get home and bring some food and matches back to the girl for tonight." Doug patted Josh on the shoulder.

Josh turned the airplane south toward the ocean and started down. He left the power setting high so the little airplane would go down fast. When the airspeed indicator got to the red line, he pulled back on the throttle so the airplane would maintain its speed.

When they got out over the strait, Josh leveled off, turned the airplane around, and started toward the little airstrip. He flew up the channel until he saw the Goose in the distance. He lowered the flaps, cut the power, and slowed the plane down so he could land when he got to the runway.

When the airplane got too low, he would put the power in and fly level, then he would pull the throttle and let the airplane settle a little. This time he passed low over the Goose and landed on the end of the runway. The plane rolled about fifty feet up the runway and stopped. Josh turned the plane around and taxied back to the cabin. He shut the plane down and jumped out. His dad crawled out of the back seat.

"Joshua, I'll go find a bucket and a long rope, and you go get some food from your mother."

Josh jogged up to the cabin. He started talking before he got into the cabin.

"Mom, the person up there was a girl!"

"A girl?"

"Yeah, she looked to be twelve or thirteen years old. She told us she was hungry. We're going to take some food and matches up to her in the airplane. Then we'll go get her on foot. What can we take her to eat?"

"Does she have anything with her?" asked Liz.

"It didn't look like it. I don't think she does. The only thing we could see was a torn up red jacket. She didn't have a fire. She was hiding in a big log when we got there. She said there were bears."

"It doesn't sound good. We have crackers and packages of smoked salmon. She probably needs some water. I'll bag up some cookies, too." Liz was getting the crackers out of the cupboard. "Joshua, you get the matches while I gather up the rest of the things."

Josh went to his bag and rummaged through his clothes. In the inside pocket he had two little boxes of waterproof matches. He took one of them out and carried it to his mother.

"Thank you, Honey. Let me put them in a plastic bag." Josh saw the tears rolling down her face.

"What's wrong, Mom?"

"That poor little girl. Out there all alone, with no food or fire, and getting troubled by a bear. Where are her parents? I'm not sure I could stay out there all alone."

"She only has to spend one or two more nights alone. Dad and I will hike up to get her after the food drop."

Doug carried a small bucket and what he called the "rescue rope." It was the rope Josh had used to pull his dad up the cliff the time he was startled by a bear and fell down to the ledge and broke his leg.

"This is the only rope we have. It might be too short and too big around, but it will have to do. I figured we needed it on the first trip here and now we need it again"

Josh just smiled. The rope was short. Josh had cut some off to tie something together. He thought they had eighty-five or ninety feet of rope. That meant he would have to fly right down on the trees. There might be some trees a hundred feet or taller. How were they going to make this work?

"That rope is short. Did you bring some parachute cord? Maybe we could tie them together."

"No, there's nothing else. Joshua, we'll make it work."

They packed everything inside the bucket and Doug kissed Liz goodbye.

"We will be back in an hour or so," said Doug.

"You boys be careful out there. Don't take any chances. That little girl needs you alive and so do I."

When they got to the airplane, they put the bucket and rope behind the back seat, and Doug crawled in.

"Dad, I think we better pray before we go."

"I thought you would never ask. Father, we need Your help in this. Give us wisdom and courage to pull this off. For Your protection we also pray. In Jesus' name, amen."

"Amen!" Josh started the airplane. He checked the oil, did the mag check, and started to taxi up the hill to the other end of the runway.

Josh was nervous about the bucket drop. He knew his dad wanted him to learn how to do it, but what if the rope wasn't long enough? What if the trees were taller than they thought?

He pushed the throttle forward and started the roll down the runway. The airplane gained speed, lifted off, and roared out over the water. When he passed the cabin, Josh looked over and saw his mom on the front porch.

At altitude he turned the airplane around to fly back up over the runway. The trail Josh had pulled his father over was now part of the airstrip and went right off the end of the runway.

"Dad, help me keep an eye on the trail. I'm not sure I can follow it because of the trees."

"Okay, Son."

When they got to the end of the runway, Josh could see the trail running off into the trees. He followed what he could see for ten minutes.

"Dad, I think we missed the Y in the trail. Do you think I should turn now?"

"Let's go on a little farther."

After five more minutes, Josh was starting to think this was going to be much harder than he had thought. They needed to get back to the girl and lower the food and matches down to her. What if they couldn't find her again?

"Joshua! There it is. The Y...off to our left."

Josh looked at the Y and then out the right window. He turned the plane to the right and traced the trail up the mountain to the summit. He started to climb, hoping to see more of the trail. The area started to make sense to Josh. He could see a ridge running to the right and a deep canyon up ahead which he thought was the place where his dad fell. But he would have to wait and see.

The trail was more visible now. When they crossed the summit it seemed to all be out in the open. Josh didn't remember any of it being out in the open. It seemed they were in the trees the whole time he was pulling the travois. But then all he could remember was the rain, clouds, and the aches and pains.

When they flew out over the deep canyon, he spotted the ledge and the broken log he had used to lift his dad. He turned the plane to the left and flew up toward the girl. The terrain was beginning to have a familiar appearance. When they crossed over the little clearing, the girl was standing out in the open, waving her arms.

"There she is, Dad."

Doug unlatched the top window on the door and pushed it out to latch it on the wing. He picked up the megaphone and stuck it out of the opening.

"Cut the power, Joshua." Josh pulled back on the throttle and the rushing wind was all they could hear.

"We brought you some food and matches."

The girl jumped up and down in excitement.

"We are going to let the food down in a bucket. If the bucket is swinging, don't get near it. Do you understand?" The girl pushed her hands up over her head.

"Joshua, we're going to make a tight right turn directly over the clearing. When you are in the turn I will let the bucket down on the rope."

Josh nodded and took the airplane over the clearing. When he got to the edge, he started to make the turn.

"Tighter, Joshua." Josh banked the airplane more and Doug held the bucket out of the window. He started to let the rope out slowly as the bucket started its long descent toward the ground.

"Joshua, the bucket is swinging. You're going to have to make a tighter turn."

Josh stepped on the rudder and pulled back on the stick. The plane seemed to be rotating around the wing. Josh wanted to see the bucket as it lowered to the ground, but the giant trees seemed to be reaching into the air trying to grab the tiny airplane. He glanced out of the side window and saw the bucket swinging wildly. The trees were real close to the wing.

"Dad! Are we too close to the trees?"

"Hang on just another minute. The bucket is settling down. It is starting to turn slowly. Just one more minute."

Josh didn't dare to look at the bucket. They were too close to the trees and it frightened him. He kept his eyes glued to them. The trees were getting closer and closer.

When they came around Josh saw the wing of the plane was going to hit one of the big spruce trees. He pushed hard on the left peddle and leveled the plane. With that done he pulled back on the stick, pushed the throttle all the way forward, and started a steep climb. The rope and the bucket crashed into the surrounding trees. The bucket tore through the trees sending tree parts crashing to the ground. The rope pulled through Doug's hands at lightning speed. His dad grabbed the rope with both hands and held on. The bucket finally cleared the trees just before the rope ran out. The girl ran and crawled into the log.

"That was close!"

"That was. This time when you get into the turn, maintain your altitude. Let's try it again."

Josh hated it when he made mistakes like that. He had endangered both of them by letting the airplane slip down in the turn. He wouldn't let that happen again.

Josh flew around in a circle, trying to calm down while his dad pulled the bucket back to the plane. When the bucket got there, Doug pulled the pine needles and branches out of the bucket and tossed them out the window. One of the bottles of water was missing.

He looked for the end of the rope and tied it to one of the braces inside the airplane, then took out his knife and opened the blade.

"Joshua, I tied the rope onto the plane and I have my knife out so I can cut the rope if anything happens."

When his dad was ready, he flew down to what he thought was a safe height over the trees. He started the turn and this time maintained his altitude.

"Okay. Here it goes." Doug started to let the rope and bucket out of the side of the airplane. He leaned out of the door as far as he could and moved the bucket down below the bottom of the plane. When it was clear, he let go of the bucket and held on to the rope.

Josh flew the airplane in a tight circle, paying close attention to his altitude.

"That's good, Son. Good flying. The bucket is going down straight."

Josh just nodded his head. He kept his mind and eyes on flying. He didn't want a repeat of what happened before. His dad let the rope down slowly.

"There's not enough rope."

"Do you want me to go down some?"

"No, don't. We're not going to be able to do this."

"How high is it off the ground?" said Josh.

"It looks to be about twenty or twenty-five feet."

"There's nothing in the bucket that will break. Can we drop the bucket?"

"We'll have to drop the rope, too. It would take too long to pull it in," said Doug.

He reached down and tried to untie the rope. The knot had tightened with the weight of the spinning bucket and the wind. Doug found the knife he had stuck under one of the braces and cut the rope.

The bucket started to fall down toward the orange tarp on the ground. When it crashed onto the ground, it tipped over, and everything went tumbling out in all directions.

Josh rolled the plane back to level flight and then circled the campsite again. After the third time around, Doug stuck the megaphone out of the window and Josh cut the power.

"The food and matches are on the ground," said Doug through the megaphone.

They watched the girl crawl out of the log and run over to the food. She looked up at the airplane and put both hands in front of her like she was thanking them.

"You have one more night. We will be back to get you tomorrow."

The girl put both hands straight up above her head. Josh put the power in, turned the airplane toward the cabin, and noticed the weather was closing in again.

CHAPTER 4

A Cessna Caravan on floats was tied up right behind the Goose. It was a beautiful airplane and Josh wondered whose it was. A man stood out on the porch talking with his mother when they passed over the Goose.

"Who was that?" Doug turned and looked out the window as the porch flashed by.

"I don't know. He has a nice airplane though."

When they got the Mountain Goat turned around, and parked, they were met halfway back to the cabin by Liz and the man. The man looked familiar to Josh, but he stepped back behind his dad. The man stepped forward with his hand held out.

"Doug Powers, I haven't seen you in ten years."

"I almost didn't recognize you without the beard."

Josh tried to think of all the people who used to have beards, but couldn't come up with anyone. If it had been ten years, he would have been only five years old, so it didn't surprise him.

"Hi, Joshua. I'm Mac. Bill MacIntosh. You can call me Mac. You grew up since the last time I saw you down in the jungle."

"Nice to meet you again," Josh said.

"Doug, I have an old guy up in Fairbanks who has two planes he wants to give away. Says he's done flying. Wants to give them to a missionary. I don't know what kind they are, but I thought you might be interested."

"We have a little girl up there on the ridge we need to rescue. She's been up there for a couple of days," said Doug.

"Honey, why don't you go with Mac. We could use the new airplanes. I'll go with Josh to get the girl," said Liz.

"That might work. What do you think, Joshua?"

Josh thought for a while. He never pictured his mother being an outdoors type of person.

"There are lots of bears out there and we are going to have to spend the night," Josh finally said. "Are you sure you want to go?"

"Joshua, I am sure. That little girl needs a mother's touch right now," she said with tears running down both of her cheeks. "Besides, I'm a jungle missionary's wife. I have been through tougher things than a hike with some bears."

[49]

"Well, that's settled then. Doug, get your gear and we'll get going," said Mac. Doug and Mac walked off toward the cabin.

"Are you sure you really want to go?" asked Josh.

"Joshua, I'm sure. It will be nice to spend time with you and see God's beauty out in the forest. Besides, that little…" She couldn't go on.

"Let's get going." He wasn't going to ask her again.

Liz reached over and took Josh's hand as they walked back to the cabin. She had already packed everything for Josh and his dad. She opened the daypack and took out his dad's extra shirt and put in a few things for herself.

"Let's go, Joshua. I'm ready. Doug, let's pray together before we go."

Doug and Mac walked over and put their hands on their shoulders. Liz started to pray before anyone could say anything.

"Dear Father, protect the little girl in the mountains. Father, make a clear way for us to go and protect us. Teach Joshua and I what You want us to know. Guide our journey today. Protect Doug and Mac. Give them wisdom about these airplanes. Amen."

After hugs and handshakes, Josh and his mom started up the runway. He hardly recognized the trail he came down the day he met Willa. He remembered how the bear had followed him down the trail and the fence that used to be near the cabin. The trees his dad had to cut down to make the runway were piled off to one side. Josh didn't know how his dad had moved some of them, but his dad had done this before. Hacking a runway out of the jungle was harder than this one.

The afternoon rain started to come in sheets that made it hard for them to see.

His mother opened his pack, pulled out a blue poncho, and handed it to him.

"Good thinking, Mom. Is there one in your pack?"

"Yes, there is. I think of everything, don't I? You're not traveling with your dad." She smiled. Josh laughed and opened her pack. The poncho was there on the top and he handed it to her.

Josh pulled the poncho over his head. The opening in the top wouldn't fit over the visor on his cap. It pushed the hat down and smashed it on his face. His arms were not in the armholes, so he fumbled around inside the poncho, trying to get free. When he finally got his head into the hood, his hat was stuck on his chest. Josh looked up at his mother.

"That was very entertaining! This trip is going to be good—real good."

"Just trying to keep the troops happy," said Josh sheepishly.

The rain started to let up a little when they got to the end of the runway. On the right side of the airstrip Josh saw the trail leading into the cloud-covered forest.

The big trees and cloud cover made Josh feel uneasy. He remembered the bear and realized he couldn't see very far, or hear anything except the rain hitting the hood of his poncho. He had to keep his attention on walking up the trail. If there was a bear, he wanted to try and frighten it away.

Josh's mother tried to talk to him, but the rain had started to fall again. Sometimes all he could hear was the roar of the rain. His mother gave up, put her head down, and walked up the trail.

The rain came in waves. One minute it rained so hard they couldn't see where they were going. Then the rain would stop and the fog would settle in. When the rain stopped, Josh thought he could hear water running. He didn't remember any water along this trail, but he was probably thinking about his dad's injuries and didn't hear the stream.

"How much farther is it, Joshua?" said his mother when the rain had stopped.

"It's about ten miles, I think. The "Y" is up at the top of this hill. We'll stop and rest there." He was worried about his mother. The rain didn't help and the hill was steep. She didn't do things like this very often. He wondered if she could make it.

All she could do was nod her head and keep sloshing along. Josh kept looking at her to see if she was all right.

"Father, protect my mother. Give her comfort and rest as we go." His prayer was drowned out by the sound of rain.

The hill started to get steeper. It went straight up the side of the mountain. Josh couldn't see the top. They put their heads down and kept climbing. The sound of rushing, rolling water was getting louder. Josh tried to figure out where the sound was coming from.

Josh knew they were almost to the "Y" in the trail. The last part of the climb was the steepest. When they got to the "Y" Josh hoped it would be easy going from there.

He turned and tried to talk to his mom. The rain made it impossible. Josh stopped and let his mom catch up.

"Mom, are you all right?"

All she did was nod and kept moving up the trail. Josh let her pass, then followed close behind. His eyes darted back and forth as he looked for a bear. He didn't know what they did in the rain, but he was leery. The bears were the big, dangerous creatures in this forest.

Josh could see the trail leading off to the right. He walked up close to his mom and tapped her on the shoulder. She stopped and he pointed up at the trail.

"This is the steepest part of the whole trip. It's uphill, but not too far."

"Good! Thank You, Lord." She started up the trail to the "Y".

The last fifty yards were the worst. When she got to the top, she stopped, and stood staring at something. Josh thought it was probably a bear. He ran as fast as he could up the steep, rocky trail. His mother didn't know what to do with a bear and he wanted to protect her.

When he got there he saw it. The trail was a river of rocks and mud rushing down around a bend. The rock crashing together was what made the sound they heard. Josh couldn't believe how loud it was.

"It's a good thing the trail is slanted. All this mud and rocks would be down on the runway."

"Joshua, which way do we go?"

"We have to go up the hill. We'll have to walk off to the side of the trail. Let's look for a place we can cross without too much trouble."

"Lead the way, Joshua."

Josh turned and gingerly made his way up the edge of the flowing brown water. He remembered the power of the muddy water in El Salvador when he dove in to avoid the black panther.

"Mom, stay close behind me and step in my footprints."

CHAPTER 5

The rain was getting worse. It would go from a hard downpour to a deluge. The noise was incredible. Between the muddy water, rocks running down the trail, and the sound of the water coming through the trees, Josh couldn't hear anything his mother said. He could barely think.

They walked for an hour beside the river through the trees. The progress was slow and steady. It was starting to get dark so Josh looked for a place for them to stop.

He wondered what the bears did in a rainstorm like this one. Did they hunker down somewhere or were they on the prowl? He looked around, trying to see one before it saw them.

They walked on for twenty more minutes before they came to the place where the river joined the trail. It came down the side of the mountain right onto the path. The problem was Josh and his mom were on the wrong side.

Josh stopped by the edge of the water. Across the raging water the trail was clear, but they had to get across the torrent. The water looked like it was six or seven feet wide. He thought about going back down the edge of the trail to a place where they could jump across, but he didn't remember seeing any. Besides, the other side of the trail was a steep canyon. He didn't know if his mom would be safe. He didn't want to risk it.

Josh started to look around for a log or something they could put across the muddy water. He walked up next to a giant spruce and took off his pack.

"Mom, I want you to sit down with your back to the tree and hold my pack. I'm going to look for a log we can use for a bridge."

His mom nodded and sat down by the tree. She looked tired to him and he was beginning to worry. She pulled the hood of her poncho down over her face as much as she could and bowed her head.

He leaned down so she could hear him. "I'll be right back."

Josh walked up the hill looking for a log to bridge the river. He saw hundreds of downed logs, but they were all too big. When he finally found the right length log it seemed too small. It was a piece of spruce about twelve feet long, eight inches in diameter, and tapered down to nothing on the other end.

"This will have to do."

Josh picked up the small end of the log and dragged it back to the water. He stood the log up on the big end and carried it over to the edge. He let the log down slow until he couldn't hold it any longer and dropped it across the water. He took two rocks and placed them on each side of the log. He had to keep it from turning.

He placed one foot on the log and bounced. It seemed springy, but he thought it would hold. He took both packs and threw them across the river. Josh got up on the log with both feet and walked across it to the other side. He picked up two more large rocks and placed them next to the log so it would not wash away.

"Mom, let's go."

Liz didn't hear him because of the roar of the rain and rush of the water. Josh stepped up on the log, balanced, and went back. He tapped his mom on the head.

"Let's go, Mom. I have a log for a bridge."

Liz pulled the hood back so she could see and held out her hand for Josh to help her up. Josh pulled her to her feet. He walked over and stepped up on the log.

Josh walked across the log. When he got to the other side he looked at his mom. She was staring at the bridge.

"Come on, Mom. You can do it."

"I can't. I can't do it." Josh couldn't hear her, but he saw her lips move.

"Mom, you can cross. It's only six feet."

This time Liz just shook her head. He walked back across the log to his mother. She reached out and hugged him.

"Mom, I won't let anything happen to you. Father, protect my mother as we cross this bridge together. Give her peace that she is doing the right thing by rescuing the girl," Josh whispered so she couldn't hear him. Josh took her hand and walked over to the log.

"Mom, follow me. Don't look at the water. Keep your eyes on me."

Josh stepped up onto the log and walked a few steps, holding his mother's hand.

"Don't look at the water. Look at me."

Liz looked at Josh and stepped up on the log. She squeezed his hand so tight it hurt. This time when Josh got closer to the other side, their combined weight made the log go underwater and muddy water covered their boots. Josh glanced back at his mom as she was watching the water spray up Josh's leg.

"Keep moving, Mom. Don't look down."

Josh jumped the rest of the way to the bank and pulled his mother with him. She tripped and fell on top of Josh, but they were safe now. They were lying in a pile on the rain-soaked ground and she started to laugh. The water that had built up behind the log pushed it crashing down the stream.

"That was exciting!" They couldn't help but laugh.

The trail flattened out and started to make a steady climb. Josh recognized where they were. They were a mile or so from the rock and it was starting to get dark. The hike had taken longer than Josh had expected.

"Mom, I think we are about a mile from where we camped when Dad got hurt. Maybe we will stay there tonight. It has a place where bears can't go."

"We haven't seen any bears yet, Joshua."

"I hope we don't either. Maybe they don't like the rain. The bear we saw was gigantic. It was about this tall on all fours." Josh held his hand up as high as his chest.

"That is big, Joshua. I hope we don't see one either. I wouldn't mind resting some. Let's go on to your campsite and rest there."

"That would be good. We have to leave the trail there and head north through the forest, then go about three quarters of a mile. I don't want to do that in the dark."

Josh started up the trail. He could tell his mother was tired, so he moved slower than he had. He kept checking on her to see if she was all right.

Liz hadn't done anything like this in years. She was happy being a missionary's wife, staying at home, raising her kids, and praying. She always prayed for her husband when he went out on a flight. And when Joshua started to fly and go places on his own that took her to her knees.

By the time they got to the rock it was almost dark. Josh took off his pack.

"I'm going down to the ledge where we camped. If it looks good, I'll come back and get you. Why don't you sit right here and rest."

He helped his mother sit down and pulled her hood up over her face. Josh crawled down the cliff to the ledge to check it out. He was surprised how much water flowed across the rock face. His dad's backpack was still laying right where he left it. He picked it up and rummaged through it to see if there was anything useful. The only thing he found was a soggy, wet flannel shirt, and a cooking kit.

Josh opened the cooking kit and took out the coffee pot. He thought his mom might enjoy a warm drink. He climbed the rocks and sat down next to his mom.

"We can't go down. We'll have to spend the night up here. There is an inch of water running across the surface of the rock." Liz looked up at Josh and smiled.

"This place is fine, Son."

"I have to gather wood before we lose the light. Why don't you wait here."

"No, Joshua. I'll help you. I can gather wood."

"Okay, but stay right around here." He was embarrassed for talking to his mother like he was talking to a child. But she was tired and he was afraid she would have a bear encounter.

Josh went off and found six long poles. He had a hard time carrying them all back to the campsite. When he got back, he was surprised by how much wood his mother had gathered. They had a large pile and even found some moss growing someplace dry.

"Look what I found," she smiled and pulled the moss and dry punk wood out of her poncho.

"Wow, that's great! It will make lighting the fire easy. Mom, do we have any parachute cord?"

"We don't have cord, but there is a roll of twine in your daypack. While I was packing and praying, the Lord told me to put the twine in. I almost didn't do it. I'm glad I obeyed. Thank You, Father."

Josh went to his pack and ran his hand around inside. There on the bottom of his pack he found a ball of twine.

"Thank You, Father, for the twine and my mother," Josh prayed silently.

He picked up one of the poles and broke it off to be about four feet long. Then he picked up a pole that was longer and laid it on top of the rock. He took the twine, tied the two pieces of wood together in a square corner, and laid them down. Josh did the same thing five feet away. His mother saw what he was doing and stood up the other end.

Josh then looked for a pole that would go between the two corners. When he found it, he laid it on top of the post and rafter his mom was holding. He tied the cross pole to the corner poles, then went to the other end and tied the pole to the corner.

"You're good, Joshua. How did you learn to make a shelter?"

Josh shrugged his shoulders, picked up a pole, and laid it on a big rock. Then he took the last three poles and laid them from the cross pole to the rock and tied them in place.

"Mom, I'm going to gather some spruce bough for our roof. Why don't you light the fire? The matches are in—"

"I have matches, Joshua. Remember, 'Don't go into the jungle without matches.'"

Josh laughed. He didn't know his father had ever said that to her, but he must have.

Josh was gone about twenty minutes and had all the boughs he needed. He had just started back to the camp when he heard an air horn and his mother yelling. He dropped the boughs and ran back to camp. His mother was standing, looking down the trail, while holding a can with a little red horn still pointed downhill.

"Joshua, there was a bear. He was huge! He didn't like the air horn though." His mom didn't turn to look at Josh.

"We better get more wood for the fire and I'll run back and get the boughs." He turned and started to run back out in the woods.

When he got back to camp, his mother had a hot fire going out in front of the lean-to. Josh piled all the boughs on the frame and tried to lay them so they would shed water down over the rock. He chuckled as he turned around and still saw his mother clutching the air horn.

Josh spent the rest of the time before dark gathering all the wood they could use and then some. He didn't want another visit from the bear.

They both crawled inside the shelter. As the evening wore on, the water started to drip inside. The heat from the fire felt good, but the dripping of the water started to get irritating. Josh got up and pulled his poncho over his head. He pulled the drawstrings on the hood to shut it off and then unsnapped the sides. He was dry down to his knees, but that would change in a minute.

He ducked out of the shelter and spread the open blue poncho on the top of the boughs. He ran around gathering little rocks to put on top of the poncho to keep it from blowing away.

When he crawled back in the shelter, he was wet and cold. He didn't think he would get as wet as he did, but now he was soaked. His mother's poncho had almost dried out from being under the shelter.

"Joshua, you're wet. Why didn't you take my poncho and put it on the top? I could have stayed almost dry down here." She took off her poncho and gave it to Josh. "Put this on and try to warm up."

Josh slipped the poncho over his head and wrapped his arms around his body. The fire was starting to feel good.

"You fixed the leaks." Josh nodded and sat, staring into the fire.

After a few minutes of silence, Liz reached over and took Josh's hand. She started to talk and then stopped. There were a few more minutes of silence.

"You know, Joshua, you were very brave today."

"I'm not a hero."

"I didn't say you were heroic, I said brave. There is a difference. When you crossed the log over the muddy, churning water you did it with such ease. I felt so proud of you and at the same time I was afraid you'd want me to cross."

"I did want you to cross."

"When I got out over the water and my heart was racing, the story of Peter and Jesus walking on the water came to mind. Peter must have felt like I felt."

There was a long pause and Josh glanced at his mother. She was staring into the fire with tears rolling down her cheeks.

"Peter must have been afraid when he was sitting in the boat, even when he said, 'Jesus, can I come to You?' Can you imagine? And then when he got out of the boat and felt the firmness of the water. That must have been something, and looking around and seeing the wind…and waves…and he stopped looking at Jesus."

"That's why I wanted you to look at me, so you wouldn't look down and see the water," whispered Josh.

"I think I laughed when we fell down because I was safe. Maybe Peter laughed when Jesus reached out, took his hand, and saved him. That's why we always have to keep our eyes on Jesus. He always saves us when we ask. No matter what is going on, we are always safe with Him."

Josh nodded his head and they sat looking into the fire. The rain had increased to a roar and the roof of the shelter started to drip. Josh took the poncho off, unsnapped it at the side, and spread part of it across his mother. She welcomed the covering and snuggled against him.

"Put your arm around me, Joshua." Josh did what his mother asked. He realized he had not put his arms around his mother in years. He felt bad about it and hoped she understood. She always seemed to understand. He hugged her a little tighter and her warmth felt good to him.

The rain stopped just like it had started. Raining one minute, then not raining the next. Josh peeked out of their shelter and was surprised to see stars through a hole in the clouds.

[65]

"Father, thank You for the rain. Give us a sunny day tomorrow. We need to find the girl. Keep her safe tonight. Amen."

"Amen," said Liz.

Liz went to the woodpile and threw some of the wood closer to the shelter. Then she threw wood on the fire and built it up into a bonfire.

"That warmth feels good."

"It's not for us. It's to keep the bears away," she said with a smile.

CHAPTER 6

The bright morning light awoke Josh from a sound sleep. He woke up several times during the night to put wood on the fire, but every time he did the fire was blazing and warm. Josh was surprised his mother was gone. He got up, stretched, and looked around. His mother walked out from behind the rock.

"There was a bear here last night," said Liz with a somber tone.

"Why didn't you wake me up?"

"I was being a mother and letting you sleep."

"You could have honked your horn," he chuckled.

"I didn't want to wake you. Besides, the bear came four times and stood outside the fire, rocking back and forth, and taking a swipe at the fire now and then."

"We better keep our eyes open today because we have to go this way." Josh pointed through the brush. "It's less than a mile."

Josh took the poncho off the top of the shelter, shook the water off, rolled it up, and stuck it in his pack. His mother got the poncho they had used as a blanket, folded it, and put it in her pack.

"Joshua, I think we better eat one of these granola bars for breakfast."

"Thanks, Mom." Josh took the bar from his mother and bowed his head.

"Father, thank You for the rain and fire we had last night. Thank You for protecting us from the bear. Help us find the girl and get her to safety. Guide our steps today. Amen."

"Amen," said his mother. "You pray just like your father. He is always thankful for the simple things in life."

That embarrassed Josh. He didn't know what to say. His face started to grow warm so he turned away. He stood there and ate his breakfast, then turned to his mother.

"Well, we better get going. If we hurry we can get up there, get the girl, and go back to the cabin tonight." Josh checked his watch for the direction like his dad had taught him. Liz rummaged around in her daypack.

"Where is that thing?" she said to herself as she ran her hand around under everything in the pack. "Ah, here it is."

Josh was still looking at his watch.

"Joshua, would you like to use this instead?" His mom held a compass out to him. "You know your father, 'Don't go anywhere without a compass.'"

Josh laughed and took the compass from his mother. His father had said the girl was directly north of them, so he set the compass to north and peered over the top at a rocky point up ahead. He could see the rock from anywhere and they needed to go a little to the right.

"We're going to go to the rock outcropping up there. It looks like it is about a half mile from here."

"Let's get going," said his mom as she set out through the brush as Josh slipped his pack on. The route they followed was not very steep and the sun had just broken over the ridge. It was a beautiful day and there was a breeze coming directly at their faces. Josh smelled a faint whiff of smoke. He looked around and didn't see any. He thought it was a burned out tree or something from last night.

His mom got a little ahead of him and disappeared.

"Mom!" Josh yelled. "Mom, wait for me!"

When Josh came over a little rise, he saw it. There in the path was a big, black bear. It stood on its hind legs and growled at his mother. He picked up a stick and put it and his other arm above his head. Josh started to scream and run towards the bear. His mother seemed to be frozen in that spot.

When Josh got beside her, she took her pack off and started to fumble around in it for her little red horn. The bear came down to all four paws and charged a few steps. It swiped the air and growled. Josh started to worry the bear might attack.

A loud blast from the horn made the bear stop. It stopped everything. It stopped growling and waving its paw. It stood looking at them. A second blast turned the bear into a clumsy giant. It couldn't get away fast enough. It looked like a frightened dog running from his attacker.

Josh and Liz stood there in silence and watched the bear disappear over a ridge. Liz put her pack on, but held on to her horn.

"Joshua, you go first."

"I was going to warn you not to get too far ahead because of the bears."

"I wish you would have. He took ten years off my life."

"Do you smell smoke?" Josh said changing the subject.

"Yes, I do. Maybe that's our girl."

"Yeah, maybe. We need to keep our eyes open for the bears and smoke."

"Amen!" said Liz.

When they got to the rock outcropping the smell of smoke was stronger.

"Mom, you stay here with your horn. If you see a bear, honk it. The bears don't seem to like it. I'm going to climb this rock to see where the smoke is coming from." Josh put his pack down and started up the rocks.

"You be careful!"

"You keep your eyes peeled for a bear. They like to follow, you know. Sit down with your back against the rock and keep a look out."

Josh climbed the rock and looked north. Off to the left, Josh saw a huge column of smoke rising gently into the still morning breeze.

"Mom! I think she is two hundred yards from here."

Josh climbed down and started off in the direction he saw the smoke. It was downhill from there so the hike was going fast. The smell of smoke was getting stronger as Josh looked through the forest to see if he could spot it.

"Mom, there it is," said Josh pointing off to his left. The trees almost hid the column of smoke, but Josh zeroed in. As he approached the clearing he started to yell.

"Hello…Hello! We are here to get you!" He stopped and listened.

"Hello…Hello." His mother repeated. "We have food for you and we know the way out."

There was no response. They wound around some more brush and came into the clearing Josh had seen from the air. But it didn't look the same. There on the ground was the littered pieces of the red coat the girl had been wearing. Down and pieces of the red material were everywhere. The orange tube tent didn't look any better. There was plenty of firewood, but the fire was going out.

Josh started over to the giant burned out log on the ground, but a low growl came out of the bushes near the open end of the log. Josh froze and his mother held up the little red horn. Like an out of control car crashing through a roadside barricade, the growling bear charged out of the brush.

Josh started to scream at the bear just as his mother started honking the shrill little horn. His mother stepped back behind a tree and Josh ran the other way and ducked behind the log. All the racket and noise confused the bear. He kept looking at both of them. Liz ran a few steps at the bear while blowing her ear-splitting horn. The bear took one swipe at the air, turned, and ran crashing into the woods.

"Boy, that was close."

"It sure was. I hope the girl is here. We need to get out of here fast," said Liz.

Josh went to the end of the log and looked in. There were bear claw marks in the black soot on the inside of the log. He could only see a few feet into the log because it was burned black inside.

"Hello. Little girl, hello! Hello. Hello!" Josh yelled, still bent over near the opening at the end of the log.

A muffled voice came from inside the log. Josh saw two boots sliding out of the log toward him. When the girl crawled out of the log, Josh was surprised. The girl was not six or seven like Josh imagined, she was fourteen or fifteen years old. The black soot on her face and clothes let Josh know she had spent a lot of time inside the log.

"Hi, I'm Megan Miller," said the girl as she held out her filthy hand to Josh. "Am I glad to see you!" Josh was surprised how professional she seemed as he shook her hand. His hands were not much cleaner than hers.

"Hi, I'm Liz Powers and this is my son, Joshua. He is the one that spotted you from the air the other day."

"Hi," Josh mumbled and looked down.

"You remind me of my brother," said Megan. "He's kind of shy, too."

"It looks like you have had trouble with a bear," said Liz.

"I would like to go. That bear has been bothering me since I got here. That's why I slept in that burned out log. I could pull my feet up so the bear couldn't reach me, and it tried," said Megan.

"Do you need to take anything?" said Josh.

"No. As you can see the bear has destroyed everything. My jacket, the tube tent, and all the food you brought me. Everything but the fire. But that isn't going so well," said Megan.

Josh walked over to the smoking fire and kicked dirt on it. Megan walked over and started to help.

"Are you the one who brought the food up to me?" she asked Josh.

"Yes, my dad and I," said Josh.

"That thing you did with the rope and bucket was clever," said Megan, trying to make conversation.

"The rope was too short though. That's why we had to drop it. Where is the rope?"

"I took it inside the log for a pillow," Megan said with a laugh. "A girl needs her comfort. I'll get the rope and then we can get out of here." She crawled back into the log, came out with the rope, and handed it to Josh.

Josh wound the rope around his arm and tied it to his daypack.

"Do you want the bucket, too?" said Megan. "It's over in that bush where the bear took it and I am not going in there to get it."

"No, the bucket can stay. Let's get going."

"Joshua, why don't you lead the way?" said Liz, clutching her little red horn in her hand.

"That horn worked really well at keeping the bear away. I wish I had thought of that," said Megan.

"It does, doesn't it? Megan, how and why are you out here in the middle of nowhere by yourself?" asked Liz as they started for the rock outcropping.

"There are seven other girls on the other side of this island. We are all a bunch of rich brats. We were at a camp that was supposed to teach us to be self-reliant and to get used to nature. Mr. Dickerson, the guy who runs the camp, started to fly over the mountain to Hoonah and his airplane started to put out black smoke," said Megan.

"Were you girls left alone there?" asked Liz.

"Not at first. Mrs. Dickerson saw the airplane smoke go behind the mountains. She took her dog and a rifle and went out to get her husband," said Megan.

"Did the airplane crash?" asked Josh.

"We don't know. It just went over the mountain, smoking. We stayed out there for a week. The girls fought over everything. After a week I decided to go get help. I tried to do the things Mr. Dickerson was trying to teach us," Megan said.

"You did a good job," said Josh.

"Yeah, not bad for a spoiled city girl," said Megan.

When they got to the rock outcropping, Josh climbed the rock, took out the compass, and sighted over the top looking for a reference point. He saw the mountain across the valley when his father was down on that ledge. Josh knew the ledge and the trail were directly north of the mountain. Josh climbed down, walked over to the women, and sat down.

"We need to go in a few minutes so we can get back to the cabin tonight," said Josh. "We don't want to spend the night out here with the bears again."

That made Megan jump to her feet. "No, we don't," she said.

Josh's mother sat on the rock, looking tired. She had been awake more than she slept the night before. That bear had worried her and she stayed awake most of the night to keep the huge fire going.

"Are you all right, Mrs. Powers?" said Megan.

"I'm fine, Megan. I was just thinking how good God is to us all. God had you signal Joshua at just the right time. God protected you and us from those bears. We prayed and God helped us find you," said Liz.

Megan looked at Liz like she didn't know what she was taking about. Josh was thankful his mom had broken the ice. Now he would feel more comfortable talking about the Lord. Josh knew all his mom had said was true and the look on Megan's face said she didn't know anything about God.

"Let's pray." Liz reached out, took Megan's hands, and bowed her head. "Father in heaven, thank You so much for protecting this brave girl, Megan, these last few days. Thank You that Joshua came along and she could signal him at just the right time. Thank You, Father, that we found her.

Protect us now as we go back to our cabin. In Jesus' name. Amen."

"Amen," Josh said softly and looked at Megan. The look on her face surprised him. She looked puzzled and had probably never prayed before.

"We better go," he said as he started toward the trail. Josh hated to leave Megan with questions, but they needed to get home and he knew God would provide a time for him to tell her how much God loved her.

The silence was beginning to get awkward. Josh wanted to say something so he said the first thing that came to his mind.

"Megan, how many girls did you say were at the camp?"

"Seven," said Megan. "One of the girls is sick or she acts sick. She got worried about being left alone and cried herself sick." That seemed to do the trick. Megan talked almost all the way back to the trail.

When they got to the trail, Josh was glad for a break. Now they could make good time back to the cabin. It should only take them a few hours to get back. If the weather held, Josh wanted to fly over to see where the camp was and maybe take out the girl who was sick. Josh started down the trail and the two women followed.

"Are you okay, Mom?"

"I'm fine now that we are back on the trail. How long have you girls been at the camp, Megan?"

"We have been out there all summer. Our parents said they wanted us to get out of our spoiled lifestyles and learn about the wilderness. The Dickerson's camp seemed like a perfect place to them. There are no cell towers, electricity, running water, or anything. In fact, we had to use an outhouse. There are only three buildings at the camp: a dorm, the house the Dickerson's live in, and the outhouse," said Megan.

"Sounds very nice," said Liz.

"What do you guys do? Do you live out here? My dad says I talk too much and I need to show interest in other people. I think he's right about showing interest in others. What do you do?" said Megan.

"We are missionaries in Central America," said Liz. Megan didn't seem to know what to say.

"What are you doing up here?" she finally said.

"We are on vacation. Joshua has a cabin up here. Isn't this a beautiful place?" said Liz. "Look at the mountains and the clouds."

The clouds. Josh had not noticed the clouds were building up over the bay. There was a dark sheet of rain falling in one area and blue sky with wispy white clouds in another. Yes, it was a beautiful place, but this weather could keep him from flying out to the camp.

The hike to the cabin was uneventful. They talked and walked and time went by fast. When they walked out of the trees onto the runway, Josh was glad to be back.

"What's this cleared off place?" asked Megan.

"It's a runway for an airplane," said Josh. "There's a couple airplanes tied up around here."

"Airplanes? You have airplanes? You must be rich, too," Megan said.

"Not hardly. We are missionaries. We live on money that God supplies," said Josh.

"But you said you have airplanes," said Megan.

"We borrowed both airplanes. Everything we have God has given to us. Our food, our clothes, our house, this cabin, God has given all of it to us. That's how much God loves us." He could tell Megan didn't understand, but now that he had told her God loved them, she was thinking. When they got to the end of the runway and the cabin, Megan was struck by the beauty of it all.

The fog had crept up the bay and was laying on the water like a blanket. Josh hoped it would stay like this until morning. If the fog was low on the water, he could take off and go up over the mountain to the camp.

"This is your cabin, Mrs. Powers? It is beautiful. Does it have indoor plumbing?" asked Megan.

"It's Joshua's cabin. And yes, it has indoor plumbing and you can take a shower. I'll give you some of my clean clothes," said Liz.

"It's a beautiful place," said Megan.

CHAPTER 7

Josh got up the next morning expecting it to be foggy and wet outside. The morning was damp, but the clouds had lifted above the tops of the mountains. It wouldn't be sunny and he would have to keep an eye on the weather. Alaskan weather had killed many good pilots who thought they could fly somewhere, but then the weather changed and caused them to crash.

After Josh had fueled his airplane, he went into the house to eat breakfast. He tried to get a bowl out of the cupboard without making a sound, but the bowls clattered together as he took one out. The one large room that was the living room, dining room, and bedrooms, made it hard to keep from waking people. A moan came from both sides of the room.

"I'm sorry, I didn't mean to wake you," Josh said. "But I really need to get going to find the camp and try to get the Coast Guard to get the girls out." Megan jumped out of bed and came over to him.

"I'll go with you. I know where the camp is," said Megan, straightening the clothes Josh's mother had given her.

"Are you sure? I'm not supposed to carry anyone who is not a pilot," said Josh sheepishly.

"Are you a good pilot? You do know how to fly, don't you?" asked Megan.

"I...I..." was all Josh got out of his mouth.

"He's a great pilot. I would trust him to fly me anywhere, in any kind of airplane," came a voice from his mother's bed.

"Let's go then. I'm ready. I could use some food though," Megan said as an afterthought.

Josh reached up and took another bowl out of the cupboard and handed it to Megan. He got some boxes of cereal from another cupboard and put them on the table.

"Megan, all we have is shelf milk—no refrigerator," said Josh as he handed her the bowl. His mom got out of bed, came over to the table, and sat down.

"Father, thank You for this food and this beautiful country. Protect Joshua and Megan as they fly to the other side of the island today. Hold the rest of the girls in the camp in Your hands and keep them safe. Amen," Liz prayed.

"Amen," said Josh kind of loud.

A soft-spoken "Amen" came from Megan as she sat with her eyes closed. Josh was surprised she prayed. The day before she stood wide-eyed while his mother prayed.

"I really hope all the girls are safe over there all alone. It must be frightening for them," said his mother.

Megan just nodded her head and kept eating her cereal. Between bites she finally said, "They're all right. If that one girl ever stopped crying."

"How'd you sleep last night, Joshua?" said Liz to change the subject.

"I slept okay. We need to get the other mattress so I don't have to sleep on the floor anymore," said Josh.

"We really need to do that before we take the Goose back," said Liz.

"What's a goose?" said Megan.

"The Grumman's Goose is the seaplane sitting out in the water," said Josh. He wondered why she hadn't seen it.

"A seaplane? You have a seaplane? Is it big? We could take that one over to rescue the rest of the girls," said Megan.

"No, we can't take the seaplane. We have to go over and look at the place to land and see what's there, and I have to ask my dad," said Josh.

"I am ready. Let's go," said Megan, reaching up and brushing her teeth with her finger. "I haven't brushed my teeth properly in…forever."

Josh finished the last two bites of his cereal and took all three bowls to the sink, walked in the bathroom, and brushed his teeth. The remark Megan made about not brushing her teeth "in forever" bothered him. He remembered not brushing his teeth when he was captured by the drug dealers and he didn't like the feeling.

"Let's get going," said Josh. He hugged his mother. "We'll be back in a while."

"Thank you so much for everything, Mrs. Powers," Megan said as she did an air kiss on Liz's left cheek.

All three of them walked out to Josh's airplane. He then helped Megan get into the backseat.

"Buckle your seatbelt and put the shoulder straps on. They all lock into the buckle," said Josh.

"This is going to be fun," said Megan.

"Put the green headset on. That is the intercom. When you want to talk, it has a voice-activated switch. Keep your feet away from the rudder pedals and don't try to move the stick. When we get in the air, I'm going to call the Coast Guard, so I won't be able to talk to you then." Josh crawled into the front seat.

He went through his checklist and started the plane. He taxied up to the base of the mountain, turned around, and did the mag check. He reached up over his head and gave the plane full flaps. When he was satisfied the airplane was good to go he bowed his head.

Father, protect us as we go over to the camp. Help me figure out a way to help. Give me an opportunity to witness to Megan. Amen.

"Are you all set?" he asked.

"Yes, I'm ready."

Josh pushed the throttle forward and the airplane started to roll. It gained speed and bounced over the rough terrain of the runway. When it got up to speed, he pulled back on the stick and the plane came up off the ground.

When he got in the air, Josh called the Coast Guard several times. They didn't respond. He wondered if his radio was not working or maybe the airbase was behind the mountains.

"Boy, this little puddle jumper doesn't take long to get off the ground. My dad's airplane takes a lot longer," Megan said.

"Your dad has an airplane?"

"Yeah, he has a jet. He never lets me sit in the cockpit, though. He always sits up there with the pilot. He doesn't know how to fly."

Josh didn't know what to say. He wanted to say something clever or smart aleck, but he couldn't think of anything. Megan kept talking about all the places she had been in the world and things she and her friends had done. She talked about being wealthy and how all their needs were met. Then she paused and sat without saying a word. After ten minutes she started up again.

"Josh," Megan said and then sat silent for a minute.

"Yes."

"Josh, you said God takes care of all your needs. Why does He do that?"

"God has promised if we seek first His kingdom, all our needs will be met."

"You mean if I seek God's kingdom He will make me richer? I don't need to be richer. I don't think I need God. I have everything."

"Do you ever do anything bad?"

"Sure, don't you?"

"Yeah, I do. The Bible calls the bad things we do, 'sin,'" he said. "The Bible also says, 'The wages of sin is death, but the gift of God is eternal life in Christ Jesus our Lord.'"

"What does that mean?"

"It means the bad things we do leads to death, but through Jesus we can have eternal life. Jesus is our gift from God."

"I don't think God could love me. I have done some really bad things in the last two years."

"The Bible also says God shows His love for us, in that while we were still sinners, Christ died for us. God loves you more than you know," said Josh.

Megan didn't say a word. Josh decided to let her think about all that before he went on. He wanted the Holy Spirit to convince her that what he said was true. Josh prayed silently for her while he flew. After another long pause, Megan began to cry.

"I want that. I want to seek God's kingdom. I don't want to die. What do I have to do?"

"The Bible says if we confess our sins and believe in our hearts, we will be saved. We don't have to die. All we have to do is pray and ask God to forgive us," said Josh.

Josh was surprised the verses he memorized in Sunday School came back to him when he needed them. He hadn't even thought about those verses for years. He must have been eight years old when a teacher made him learn them. He knew God was at work there in the airplane.

"I can't get on my knees in this airplane. I don't know what to say. Do I have to close my eyes?"

"You don't have to get on your knees or close your eyes. God hears you whenever you pray. Say something like this: Dear Father, I am a sinner. Please forgive me. I need—"

Josh was interrupted when Megan repeated the exact words. He waited for her to finish and then he went on.

"I need You. I need You to take over my life. Thank You that Jesus died on the cross for me. Thank You for saving me. In Jesus' name. Amen," Josh said. Megan repeated every word.

"Is that all? Did I say enough, Joshua?"

"That's all there is to it."

"What do I have to do now?"

"Well, you have to stop doing the bad things you were doing, read your Bible every day, pray, and do whatever the Bible and God tells you to," said Josh.

"I don't have a Bible."

"I'll get you one," said Josh as they came out over the west coast of the island. "Which way do we go?"

Megan looked out both sides of the airplane. She thought awhile then said, "We go right."

"Are you sure?"

"Yes, I am sure," was all she said.

Josh banked the airplane right and started to fly up the coast. It was a beautiful island on a beautiful day. The clouds were high and broken, and the blue sky was breathtaking.

"You better look outside and tell me when we get to the bay."

Megan didn't say anything, but turned to the right and looked out the window. They flew in silence and passed one bay after another. Finally, they came to a small bay that looked like it was a mile long.

"That's it! That's the bay. Turn right. The camp is on the left side of the bay. Fly up and look. I'll show you where you have to land."

Josh turned into the bay and flew over to the left side. They flew halfway up the bay before they came to the buildings.

"There it is right there," said Megan. "Do you see the tracks of Mr. Dickerson's airplane there on the sand? We walked the full length of the runway looking for big rocks that would damage the plane. It's a safe place to land."

Josh pulled the power off and slowed the plane, then pulled the handle to full flaps. He increased the power enough to carry the airplane down towards the ground. When he was lined up with the beach, he let the plane settle into a slow descent to the ground. The airplane touched down and rolled to a stop.

He put the power in, turned the plane around, and taxied back toward the buildings. When he got up near one of the buildings he shut the plane down.

"Here's the girls," Megan said.

Josh looked out of the airplane and almost laughed. Two of them were dressed like they were at the beach. They had on sunglasses, sweatshirts, flip-flops, and shorts. Another was dressed like an Eskimo with a hood and very thick, furry boots. The fourth one was dressed like a supermodel at a fashion show with high heels. The last one was standing off to the side by herself and dressed like a normal girl on a camping trip.

"That's an interesting group," said Josh, looking down and smiling.

"You don't know the half of it."

Josh got out of the plane first and walked around to the girls. He really didn't know what to say. He just stood there and waited for Megan. The girls all stared at Josh like they had never seen a boy before.

When Megan walked around the edge of the airplane all the girls stared at her.

"Megan, where did you get those clothes? They're not very stylish," said the model.

"Josh's mother gave them to me. Mine were filthy. Where is Shelly?" said Megan.

All the girls started to talk at once.

"Be quiet!" yelled Megan. That seemed to calm them down.

"Where's Shelly?" Megan asked again.

"She's sick," said the supermodel. "Who is this dreamboat that flew you out here?"

"Oh, this is Josh. These are the girls," said Megan. "How sick is she?"

The model seemed to talk for all of them. She stepped forward and struck a pose with her feet apart and one hand on her hip. Josh almost laughed out loud so he turned around and walked over to the plane.

"Shelly has been in bed crying since you left. She only eats a bowl of soup that Sarah feeds her," said the model. The two beach girls rolled their eyes and one of them stepped forward.

"She's faking," said the girl. She wants us to wait on her. She never wanted to be here in the first place."

"And you did?" asked the model in a sarcastic tone.

"Girls! Let's go see her and talk about what we're going to do next," said Megan as she started for the cabin. All the girls turned and trudged up toward one of the buildings.

Josh decided to tag along so he got in line behind the girls. When they were halfway to the cabin the girl dressed in normal camping clothes came back beside him.

"Hi, I am Sarah. You're Josh, right?" said the girl.

"Yeah, Josh Powers," he said.

"Sarah Van Den Mouller," she said and held out her hand for Josh to shake. "She's not really sick, you know. She has been crying off and on since we got here. She wants to go home. So do I, but not for the same reasons. I miss my family."

Josh nodded as they walked into the dorm. It looked like a bomb had gone off in it. There were suitcases opened, clothes all over the floor, and a big pile of trash in one corner. The only neat place in the room was Sarah and Megan's corner and beds. It was impossible to walk through the room without stepping on something.

"You guys!" said Megan. "It didn't look like this when Mrs. Dickerson was here. What happened?"

"I never have to clean my room at home. Why should I do it here?" said one of the beach girls.

"You should," came out of Josh's mouth.

"You stay out of this, you…you pilot," said the girl.

Josh could feel the anger rising in his body. He wanted to say something to the girl, but walked out on the porch instead. He thought about walking out to the airplane, flying back home, and forgetting about them. But that was not how his parents raised him. These girls were in trouble and he came to help. He stayed outside until he cooled down.

Megan started yelling at the girls. He couldn't hear what she was saying but he was glad he was outside. When Josh walked back into the room she said, "Josh came to help us. Can you be nice to him?"

"Sorry," the beach girl said, not looking at him.

Josh knew she wasn't really sorry so he just looked at her and nodded his head.

"Let's see this sick girl," Josh said. "Maybe I need to fly her out today."

Under a pile of clothes on a lower bunk came a painful moan. Megan and Sarah went to the bunk and pulled all the clothes off the bed. Under the blankets they found the girl. She was pale and acted like she was in a coma. All she did was moan. Megan put her hand on her shoulder and gently shook it.

"Shelly, wake up. Are you all right?" said Megan. "Shelly." There was no response except a moan.

"I told you she was sick," said the model striking another pose.

"Do you want me to fly her out?" said Josh.

All the girls started talking at once and crowded around Josh. They all wanted to go and get back to civilization. Megan and Sarah were standing in the back not saying a word.

"Girls!" shouted Megan. "If Shelly is sick Josh can fly her out. He knows where we are and will send help for us."

Megan tried again to wake Shelly. The moans were the only sound she made. Josh decided he had better take charge and fly the girl to safety.

"Help me get her to the plane," he said. All the girls turned around and walked away except Megan and Sarah. The two girls wrapped her up in one of the blankets. Josh went to her head and shoulders, one of the girls took the middle, and the other her feet. When they lifted her, she was heavier than he thought she would be.

"Can a couple of you girls give us a hand?" Josh said.

"No. She's faking. I'm not going to help her," was all that was said.

Josh shook his head and started for the door. Megan and Sarah followed along stumbling over all the stuff on the floor. When they got to the porch, one of them sighed. All three of them knew it would be easier to walk the last hundred feet to the airplane.

Next to the airplane, Josh stood her up and told the girls to hold her. He went around to the other side of the plane, reached through the window, and took her shoulders. He lifted the best he could, but noticed Shelly helped herself get in despite still seeming to be in a coma.

Josh started the airplane and taxied down to the end of the makeshift runway. He pulled the lever to extend the flaps for a short field takeoff. He put the power in and started his takeoff roll. The airplane rolled down the beach and was in the air in a hundred feet. Josh kept up a steady climb until it was safe for him to release the flaps.

"Ha! I knew I could fool those airhead girls and you. I knew I could get off that island," came a voice in Josh's intercom.

CHAPTER 8

Josh spun his head around and looked at the back seat. There was Shelly sitting up and smiling with a mean grin. She had the headset for the intercom on. Josh hadn't bothered to put the headset on her because he thought she was unconscious.

"You scared me," said Josh.

"Yeah, I wanted to," was all she said.

"You were faking? I thought you were in a coma or something."

"I fooled all those people for weeks. They all thought I was sick."

"Not all of them."

"Sarah was easy. She thought I was sick and kept feeding me soup. I didn't even have to get up. While all the girls were outside, I'd get up and go to the bathroom and shower and stuff," she said.

"Sarah said you were faking. She was just helping you out."

"Why would she do that? Sarah was a selfish creep just like the rest of them."

"Maybe she wanted to serve you," said Josh.

"Serve me? Maybe my parents would hire her as a servant if that's what she wants. All you people are easy."

"What about Megan? She went off into the wilderness trying to get someone to rescue you when the Dickerson people left."

"Megan is a show-off. She thinks she knows everything. She thought she could rescue all of us. What a chump."

"Megan is a nice girl who was only trying to help."

"She's a user, just like me. She found you didn't she, Mr. Pilot?" Shelly sneered.

"No, I found her. She was out in the wilderness for a week without food or water. A bear was attacking her at night. The bear shredded her jacket and kept clawing at her hiding place. When we got her she was tired and dirty. That doesn't sound like a user to me."

"She sure fooled you," laughed Shelly.

"What's with you people? Someone tries to help you and all you do is criticize."

"Are you a goody two-shoes or a religious freak?"

"Yeah, I am. God doesn't want us to treat people like you do. God wants us to think about good and true things."

"My dad says people like you are weak. People who need God are kidding themselves. My dad says the people who trust in God are—"

"What do you think? Your dad has all these opinions. What do *you* think?" Josh interrupted.

"My dad says…I…I think…oh, just be quiet! Just don't say another word! You…you pilot!"

Josh decided to do what she asked. He turned his attention to his radio and tried to call the Coast Guard again. They still did not respond.

Father, I can't seem to get through to this girl. Make a way for me to witness to her about Your love. Convict her of the things she says and does. Amen.

The rest of the trip was done in silence. He glanced at the back seat only to be met by the ugly face Shelly made at him.

When they came down over the ridge and started to fly down the channel, Josh was glad this trip was almost over. The tension in the airplane made him sorry he volunteered to fly her out. He should have left her and brought someone else.

"We're here," said Josh as he prepared to land.

"We're where? This is not a town. This is just as bad as the place we left. This is nowhere!"

"This is our cabin. My mother is here. She will take care of you."

"I don't need your mother to take care of me. Take me to a town."

Josh reached down and shut off the intercom. He didn't want to hear anything else from this ungrateful girl. He was going to be glad to get her out of the airplane. He didn't know how his mother was going to handle this girl.

He was beginning to feel good about landing at their little homemade airport. Every time he landed it got a little easier. The plane came in over the Goose and touched down on the ground. He looked toward the back seat and Shelly was still talking at him.

When he taxied back to his parking space and pulled up between the chocks, he checked the back seat to see if she was still talking. To his surprise she looked like she was in a coma again. She was lying in the back seat limp with her head laying over against the side of the plane.

Josh switched the intercom back on. "It's not going to work this time. You already told me you were faking," he said as he turned the engine and the master switch off. He climbed out of the plane and left the door open. "I'm not going to carry you again. I am going to leave the door open and you can come in when it gets dark and bears come around." She didn't move a muscle. "Suit yourself," he said as he walked toward the cabin.

"Hi Honey. You're home a lot sooner than I thought you would be. Is everything all right?" said his mother.

"Yeah. I brought a girl that acted like she was in a coma, but she was faking," said Josh.

"Where is she?" asked his mother.

"She talked my ear off on the way here, but when I landed she went back to her act of being sick. She even made us carry her out to the airplane because she wouldn't respond to anything," said Josh. "I think she wants us to carry her in. I told her she will get out when the bears show up."

"Are you sure she is all right?"

"She's fine. Where's Dad? I thought he would be back by now," said Josh.

"You know your dad. If he has an airplane to look at he looks over every inch of it. I don't think he'll be back tonight or maybe even tomorrow."

"We have to get those girls out of there. I tried to call the Coast Guard, but couldn't get anyone. There might be something wrong with the radio in the plane. I wanted Dad to fly the Goose over and pick them up. That would be a perfect airplane for the job."

"Well, we had better wait until tomorrow. Maybe your father will be back. Let's just wait and see. Joshua, I better go check on that girl. I'm getting worried."

Josh followed Liz out to the airplane. There in the plane Shelly was sitting up and looking around. When they got halfway out the girl looked like she slipped back into a coma. Josh laughed.

"I told you she was faking and wants us to get her out of the plane."

"I'll talk with her," said Liz.

"Good luck," Josh said with a big smile on his face.

He went to the left wing and tied it to the bucket of cement. Then he walked around to the right side where his mother was talking to the girl.

"Shelly, it's not going to do any good to pretend you can't hear me. It's an hour until dark and we have a tremendous problem with bears. I'm going to leave you here until you get out on your own and come into the cabin," Liz said in a very kind voice.

Josh tied the other wing of the plane to the block and started back to the cabin.

"That girl is really something, isn't she?" said Josh.

"Nothing I can't handle. I had a sister like her."

When they got to the bottom of the steps on the front porch they heard a crash and looked back toward the plane. Shelly had crawled out of the plane and slammed the door shut. She spun around and came stomping toward Josh and his mother. Shelly started talking before she got to them.

"No one does what I want. No one even cares about me," said Shelly as she stomped her foot.

"Shelly, we care. Why do you think we went out to get you?" said Liz. Shelly didn't say anything. She stood staring at Liz with one hand on her hip.

"I want to go in the house. When can I go to town and call my dad?"

"We have to get the rest of the girls, then I'll personally take you to town," said Josh. "But we have to get the rest of them here. We have to wait for my dad."

"See? No one does what I want. Go pick up the girls, you…pilot. Hurry so I can call my dad," Shelly said as she turned and stomped into the cabin. Liz and Josh followed her inside.

"Oh great! This is worse than Camp Wildwood. There's only one room. I don't share a room with anyone," she said.

"Whatever!" Josh said.

"Joshua, you be nice," said his mom.

"Mom, this girl is—"

"Joshua. Stop," his mom interrupted. Josh turned around and walked out on the front porch. He thought about what he had said and he felt bad.

Father, forgive me for my anger and please give me patience. Help me to treat Shelly with love and respect. Amen.

"Do you have a bathroom or do I have to use the outhouse like the other horrible place?" Shelly shouted.

"Young lady, that will be enough. You have to stay with us so make the best of it. The bathroom is right there. Don't stay in it too long; others might want to use it," Liz said.

"A curtain? That's all the privacy I get? What's wrong with you people?" snapped Shelly.

"You can use the outhouse out by the trees. It has a door," said Liz.

Josh heard a big sigh and stomping across the floor.

"Mom, I'm going fishing," said Josh as he picked up the fishing pole and tackle box and walked off the porch.

"Be back about dark. I'll have dinner ready. Everything but the fish," said Liz.

"Good luck," Josh said.

"I'll be all right."

Josh walked down to the Goose and stood there for a minute looking out at the water. He was overwhelmed by the beauty of Alaska. A low fog was creeping up the channel and there was a cool breeze blowing off the water. Josh walked down the shore out of sight of the cabin.

He found a fallen tree, set the tackle box down, and went to the water's edge with the fishing rod. He watched the still water as he took the hook off the eye on the rod. He turned around, opened the tackle box, and took out an orange plastic worm that was the bait for trout. He stuck the worm on the hook, pulled the rod up over his shoulder, and cast out into the water. There was a loud plunk as the weight struck the surface and sent out rings of water.

Josh was glad he decided to go fishing, especially since it was a way to escape that girl. He closed his eyes and prayed silently.

Father, help Shelly see we are only trying to help. Give my mom something to say to her that will get her attention and bring her to You. Thank You, Father, for these beautiful—

Josh was interrupted by the reel on his fishing pole. "I got something," Josh said as he pulled up on the rod and started to crank the reel. Josh didn't expect to catch a salmon on trout bait, but he did catch something.

It was easy to crank the small fish in and when it got to the shallow water Josh saw that it was a herring.

"Good! Salmon bait," said Josh.

Josh pulled out his knife and split the herring from the tail to the middle. Then he took the hook and the leader off the rod at the swivel and threaded the line through the opening in the herring, pulling the line out through its mouth. When the treble hook was in the slit in the back of the fish, he closed the flesh around the hook and reattached it to the swivel.

Josh walked back out to the water and cast the herring and weights far out into the water. He slowly started to crank the herring back in. It had to look like it was alive and swimming.

Thirty seconds into his cranking the fight was on. His pole bent over and the reel started to whine. This was not another herring. It was the biggest fish he had ever hooked.

Josh fought the fish for forty minutes. He would get it right up next to the shore only to have it turn and start to run. Then the fish would stop moving altogether. Josh would think he lost it, but if he moved the reel just a little the battle would start all over again. That happened five times.

On the sixth trip to the shore, Josh backed up and gently pulled the fish up on the rocks, dropped the pole, and ran to grab the fish. The fish flipped over and Josh followed it into the water, straddling it with his legs. He was wet up to his waist and the water was freezing cold, but he had his fish.

While he was sitting on the fish, he reached down and stuck the fingers of both his hands into the gills of the fish. The fish that came up out of the water was half as long as him.

"Wow, this is a big fish. Wow," Josh laughed as he spoke.

Josh picked up the fish and carried it to the front porch of the cabin. He staggered up the steps with it cradled in his arms.

"Mom, come and look at this!" Josh yelled to his mom.

Josh gently kicked the bottom of the front door with his foot. His mom came to the door and pulled it open.

"Mom, look at this!" he said with a big smile on his face as he stepped into the cabin.

"That's gross. I'm not going to eat that. You'll have to make me something else to eat for dinner," said Shelly from the bottom bunk where she was sitting. Josh and his mother both looked at her.

"What? That's gross," she said again.

"Joshua, take it outside to the fish cleaning table and get it ready. I'll cook it for dinner. That is a beautiful fish."

Josh went out to the table beside the cabin and laid the fish down. He thought he better go get the tackle box and pole he had left by the water. When he got around the edge of the trees there was a bear. It was rummaging through the tackle box. Josh froze and his heart began to race. The bear looked up when he heard Josh coming.

The bear raised his head and stared at Josh for a long time. Josh backed up slowly and then stepped behind a tree. He looked on the ground for something to make himself look bigger. He picked up a large tree branch, put it over his head, and jumped out from behind the tree. Before he could start yelling the bear yelped, jerked his head out of the tackle box, and shook his head violently.

The bear had a giant treble fishhook stuck through his lip with a big lure slapping him in the face when he shook his massive head. Josh took advantage of the bear's situation and started to run toward him yelling.

"Bear, go! Get out of here, bear!" shouted Josh. The bear glanced at Josh, growled, and ran off into the woods, shaking his head and whining. Josh could hear the bear crashing through the forest.

When he got back to the cabin with the tackle box and fishing pole, his mother was standing on the porch.

"You see a bear?" asked his mom.

"Yeah. The bear got a big hook through its lip and ran off," he said. "I bet that hurts."

"I hope the bear is all right. Kind of hard to help a big wild animal with something like that."

"Maybe that will teach him not to bother people who are fishing," said Josh.

He went to the cleaning table and pulled out the large filleting knife that was stuck in the back of the table. He cut the head and tail off and slit the body of the fish down the belly. After he cleaned out the guts, he took the head, the tail, and the entrails out in the woods and threw them as far away from the cabin as he could. Then he turned on the faucet over the table and washed the fish. Josh carried the fish to his mom and set it on the kitchen counter.

"Joshua, why don't you take a shower and get some dry clothes. By then the fish will be done and we can eat," his mom said.

Josh went to his bag, pulled out some dry clothes, and went into the bathroom to shower. When he came out his mother had set the table: a tablecloth, napkins, matching dishes, and a vase of flowers.

"Where did all of this stuff come from?" asked Josh.

"You know I have to take a few things with me. I'm going to leave these things here so it will be nice every time we come. Let's eat, everyone. Joshua, you sit there and Shelly, you sit here by me," said his mom as she pointed to the chairs.

Josh sat down and waited for Shelly to come. His mother took the bread off the counter, got a sharp knife, and brought them to the table.

"What did you make me to eat?" said Shelly.

"Let's pray and be thankful, and then I'll get to that," said Liz. "Joshua, would you pray for us?"

Josh bowed his head. "Father, thank You so much for this beautiful day. Thank You that I could catch a fish for us to eat. Thank You we were able to bring Shelly here safely. Amen."

When they opened their eyes, Shelly was looking at both of them like they were crazy.

"Who were you talking to? No one was listening to you. My dad says—" Shelly stopped herself. "What did you make me to eat? I am not eating that gross fish."

"Shelly, we are having salad, homemade sourdough bread, and the salmon steaks. You can eat salad and the bread if you don't want the fish," said Liz.

"Gross!" Shelly said as she got up, stomped back to the bunk, and laid facing the wall.

Josh sat there staring at his plate. He didn't know what to say. He didn't know anyone could be so unthankful. He finished his dinner, not saying a word, and sat back in his chair.

"Mom, I'm going outside for a little while. I'll be back in a while," he said. His mom just nodded her head.

"Thank you for dinner, Mom. It was really good," he said when he got to the front door.

His mother looked up at him and smiled. He didn't want to leave his mom with that girl, but he figured she would know what to say.

Josh walked out on the front porch and stood there looking out at the Goose. Slowly, he walked down the stairs and out to the dock where it was parked. He took ahold of the wing and stood there with his hands above his head.

"Father, I don't understand why Shelly doesn't want to hear Your gospel. You know she uses the excuse, 'My dad says' all the time and doesn't think for herself. Give me the right thing to say to her so she will believe in You. Let me be an example of—" He was interrupted by his mother's soft voice.

"Joshua, you know even young people can have a hard heart and will never listen to you. Shelly has baggage, a lot of input from her father, and their wealth is probably crippling her," said his mom. "We need to keep praying for her. Let's go inside and get out of this cold."

Josh put his arm around his mom as they walked back to the cabin.

CHAPTER 9

When Josh opened his eyes and stretched, his back hurt from sleeping on the floor. He didn't want to sleep near Shelly so he had slept next to his mother's bed.

"Joshua. Joshua. Are you awake?" whispered his mom.

"I think I am," said Josh.

"Joshua, I woke up about three o'clock this morning worrying about those girls out there. Joshua, you have to go get them this morning. I don't think they should spend another day out there alone," said his mom. "I have prayed for them for two and a half hours."

"What time is it?" said Josh.

"It's about 5:30. If you got going you could have them all picked up by noon in your little airplane."

"Or, I could fly the Goose out there and pick them up all at once. Dad took me up in it the other day. I think I could fly it and land it."

"You think you can fly that plane?"

"There are enough seats for everybody and it would be a learning experience for me."

"A learning experience? I don't want you to be learning with those girls in the plane," said his mom. "I worry enough when you are by yourself. I'll be on my knees praying the whole time you are gone."

"Mom, I can fly the Goose. I just have to pay attention on the landings," said Josh sheepishly.

"All right. But, Son, you be careful. You pay attention like you said."

That was what Josh wanted to hear. He crawled up off the floor and stretched his aching body.

"I think I would rather sleep on the ground than this floor. At least I could make dents in the ground so my body wouldn't hurt so much."

Josh gathered up his clothes and went into the bathroom. When he came out, his mother had a bowl of oats ready for him to eat. He walked over to the table, picked up the bowl, drank the oats, and set the bowl down.

"I have some oats—" his mom said as she turned around just when he finished them off.

"Thanks for breakfast, Mom. Those oats were real good," Josh said with a big smile on his face. His mother just shook her head. "I better get to the weather briefing," he said as he walked out the front door.

"I'll come down to the plane before you go. Wait for me," said Liz.

Josh walked off the front porch into the most beautiful day. The sky was a blue like he had never seen. There was not a cloud anywhere. The water looked like a mirror, reflecting the images of the mountains and trees.

"Father, thank You for this beautiful day. Help me fly this airplane. Please protect the passengers. Amen."

He opened the door of the Goose, crawled in, and made his way up to the pilot's seat. He sat looking at the instruments, trying to familiarize himself with the layout. He reached into the pocket on the side of the plane and pulled out the checklist. The first thing he did was turn on the master switch to see if he had enough gas to fly over to the camp to get the girls back safely. Without gas he wouldn't be able to go. He was relieved to see there was more than enough.

Josh turned off the master switch and methodically started down through the checklist. When he got to the engine primer, he stopped. He crawled through the crawlspace under the dashboard to the nose of the plane and opened the hatch. Carefully, he crawled out onto the rocking and bobbing nose of the airplane. From there he scampered up to the top of the wing and over to the left engine. He opened the hatch on the cowling and pulled out the dipstick.

He did the same thing to the other engine. Satisfied with the amount of oil in both engines, he slowly crawled back to the nose, let himself back inside, then closed and locked the hatch. Josh crawled out of the plane and walked up to the left engine. He reached down and pulled the propeller through until the right engine was free of its oil lock.

The right engine was out over the water, so he untied the plane and tried to turn it around. The plane was heavier than he had imagined and it was difficult for him to turn by himself. It almost pulled him into the water. Struggling, he finally got it turned enough so he could grab the right wing and swing the plane around so the right engine was over the dock. He tied the airplane to the ramp and pulled the engine through.

"I saw you struggling to turn the airplane around. Wait a minute and I will be out there to help you turn it back around," his mother called from the front porch of the cabin.

Josh waved his response to his mother and sat down on the dock. He hoped that he could find the inlet on the other side of the island. He may have to fly up a few to find the camp and the girls.

When his mom came out of the cabin she walked up to him, put her arms around him, and closed her eyes.

"Oh, Father. You know sending Joshua off on this trip is scary to me. I ask that You give him all the wisdom and the know-how he needs to make this trip safe. Protect the young girls he is going to pick up. Give me peace and guard my heart and mind in Christ Jesus. I pray this in Jesus' name. Amen."

"Amen," said Josh. "I better get going before the weather changes."

"You get in the plane and I'll hold it until you are ready to go," his mom whispered.

Josh untied the airplane and started to turn it back around. His mother helped him move it slowly until the door was back by the ramp. He hugged his mom and crawled into the airplane. His mom stood on the ramp holding on to the left wingtip.

When he got to the pilot's seat and buckled himself in, he picked up the checklist and finished it. He primed the right engine, then reached up over his head, set the throttle, and pushed the starter button. The engines turned over slowly a few times, backfired, and belched out a big cloud of white smoke.

Josh let the smoke clear, then hit the starter button again. The starter whined and the engine turned over three more times and then started. He advanced the throttle as his mom let go of the pontoon and the airplane started out into open water.

He pulled back on the right throttle and pushed the left throttle forward to the starting position. Josh hit the starter button and the engine turned over twice and started like it was already warm. He pointed the airplane down the channel, reached up over his head, put the flaps down, and pushed the throttles forward so he could check the mags. With the mags checked, he looked out the side window to see what was ahead as he pushed the throttles forward to full power.

The airplane seemed to be waddling through the water so Josh waited for it to gain more speed. Then he pushed the control wheel forward and lifted the tail to get it on the step. The plane seemed to be sliding on a piece of glass as it traveled across the water. Josh held the control wheel where it was and let the plane gain speed. When it reached eighty-five miles per hour it lifted off the water.

The early morning air was smooth and the sky was bright and clear. Josh was glad he was flying west to avoid the bright light of the morning sun. He gently started the plane on a slow climbing turn. When he got to his heading he continued to climb over the mountains behind his cabin. He knew if he flew straight across the island he would come out somewhere near the camp and the girls.

When he came up over the last mountain range, the vast Pacific Ocean lay ahead. As he crossed the coastline, he slowly turned the airplane to the right and flew up the shore. Every time he came to a bay he looked to see if that was where he should turn.

Josh flew on for what seemed like too long, so when he spotted another bay he turned the airplane into it. Immediately, he knew he chose wrong. The bay was short and narrow. There was not enough room for him to turn around. He pushed the throttles forward and pulled back on the control wheel so the plane went into a steep climb. The mountain at the end was coming fast. He didn't know if he was going to make it. His heart started to race as the giant trees loomed closer.

Josh saw a low spot on the ridge just off to his right, so he turned and headed for the slot in the ridge. He could feel the airplane starting to slow from the steepness of the climb.

"Lord, I need Your help!" Josh prayed. "Come on airplane. Just a little longer."

Just as the stall warning horn sounded, Josh cleared the last giant tree that was reaching up to rip the plane from the sky. He pushed the nose down and dove into the next cove. The plane started down with a roar so Josh pulled back on the throttles and leveled the airplane off.

"That was close! I'll never do that again."

When he got out over the ocean, he made a long sweeping turn, trying to relax. This time he was more cautious, looking intently at every cove and bay. When he got to one he thought was it, he made a tight turn over the ocean and checked out the bay.

Josh circled around looking for the small beach where he landed the day before. There was a clear place but he wasn't sure it was the one. He circled around again the other way and spotted one of the cabins at the camp.

He turned out over the ocean to get a clear shot at the landing. This was the part that worried him the most. He wanted to land short so he could float the plane up to the land and taxi up onto the beach.

Josh pulled the power off. The airplane started to sink fast. He pushed the throttles a little forward. He reached over and put the flaps down twenty percent. He was going to fly the plane down to the water, let it settle on the water, and then cut the power.

When he saw the buildings flash by his window, he realized he was too high and too fast. He would never land where he wanted to. As he looked up the cove he also realized he would never be able to abort this landing. He had to get the plane down fast.

He pulled back on the throttles and let the plane fall fast. As the water was coming up, he pushed the throttles forward and tried to catch the plane before it hit. The plane slammed down on the water and skipped off like a thrown rock. It went back up into the air so he had to land again.

The end of the cove was coming up fast. Josh held the plane level and eased back on the throttles until it started to sink. He held his breath and the plane came down to the water and touched. When it was on the water he cut the power. He knew he was not supposed to do that, but he had to or he would crash onto the beach.

The airplane's nose went up so high, Josh could only see the sky. He was glad the plane was watertight. The wave he made when he hit the water came rushing from behind and pushed him toward the shore. Josh put the landing gear down so if he hit the beach at least he would roll up on the dirt. With the wheels down the plane stopped in the water. Twenty more feet and he would have been on the gravel.

Josh pushed the left throttle forward, stepped on the right rudder pedal, and turned the airplane around. To his surprise he couldn't see the camp, so he decided to taxi back. He wasn't going to take off and go through that again. He put the wheels back up and started the long trip back down to the cove.

When he was halfway down the inlet he saw one of the cabins through the trees and movement on the beach.

"That must be the girls."

Turning the plane, he started to taxi toward the cabins. When he got near the shore, he put the wheels down and the airplane slowed. He decided he should try to get the plane straight up on the beach. The beach was steeper than Josh thought and he had to push the throttles almost all the way forward. The engines roared as the airplane moved slowly up on the small rocks that made up the beach.

The plane finally broke free of the water and started to move with ease across the land. Josh pulled back on the throttles, stepped down on the left rudder, and turned the plane around. With the plane now facing the water, he shut both engines down and looked out the window. There standing in a line were most of the girls. Megan and Sarah walked up to the side of the airplane near the pilot's window as Josh slid it open.

"Hi, are you guys ready to go?" asked Josh.

"Josh, I am sooo ready," said Megan.

"Me, too. How is Shelly?" said Sarah.

The conversation was interrupted by all the other girls. They came up and started to talk all at once. Josh let them talk, got up, and walked back to the door where the group met him and continued their jabbering.

"Wait a minute!" Josh shouted as he jumped down to the ground. He was surprised by the dark clouds that had come up over the mountain. The blackness of the clouds meant rain.

Josh held up his hand. "Ladies! Ladies! Stop talking all at once and I will answer you."

The girl that was all dressed up, stepped forward and the others stopped talking. "When are you going to get us out of this miserable place? We are in a hurry to get back to civilization."

Josh couldn't help but smile. Here they were in the middle of the Alaskan wilderness and this girl had on a dress, high heels, sunglasses, and a faux mink stole.

What is this girl thinking?

"There's a storm coming and we can't fly in it," said Josh. "We have to wait for it to blow over."

The dressed-up girl took two steps forward, placed her hands on her hips, and said in a very condescending voice, "The airlines fly in the rain. Why can't you?"

"I'm not an airline pilot—" Josh was interrupted by lightning striking a nearby tree. The thunder was deafening and their hair reacted to the electricity.

All the girls started to scream and run in every direction, except the girl in high heels. She stood frozen in one place screaming. The sudden downpour caught everyone off guard. Josh stepped under the wing of the airplane and Sarah and Megan joined him. Everyone else was running around looking for a place to avoid the rain.

The dressed-up girl was standing in one spot and was soaking wet. Even her faux mink looked like a drowned rat.

"Somebody help me!" she wailed.

Josh walked out from under the wing and took her arm. Her high heels made her trip and stumble on the rocky ground. When he got her under the wing, she jerked her arm away from his grasp and pretended like she had walked over by herself.

"You're welcome," Josh said and smiled.

The girl just stared at him. "Whatever!" she said in a sarcastic tone.

Josh walked over to Megan and Sarah. "I think we better round these girls up and get them back to the cabin, at least until it stops raining and clears up. It might be a while; it might even be all night."

Megan nodded and walked out from under the wing. "Girls! Girls! Come here!"

When all the rain-soaked girls were assembled, she said, "We have to go back to the cabin, get some dry clothes, and wait for this rain to stop. When the rain stops and it is clear, Josh will fly us out of here."

Josh stood there as the girls started to mumble and walk off toward the cabin. The rain clouds had moved down onto the surface of the ground, so it was hard to see even a few hundred yards. He would be glad when he had these girls back to safety.

Josh stood under the wing until the girls had gone about twenty yards. The dressed-up girl slipped and tumbled to the ground. Her scream was deafening. Josh started to go get her but Megan and Sarah got there first.

"We got her. Are you coming, Josh?" Megan said as they got on each side of her and helped her to her feet.

"No. I think I am going to stay here until the storm blows over," he said.

"Okay. Sarah and I will be back in a little while to find out your plans for getting us out of here."

He watched as the three girls walked slowly back to the cabin. "At least that girl will get the mud washed off," he said to himself.

The storm didn't blow over. It got worse. The wind was howling. Josh thought it was blowing like a hurricane, but he knew they were too far north for that. He was glad he hunkered down in the airplane. He got out one of the survival sleeping bags that were stored in the tail compartment of the airplane, spread it out on the floor, and sat with his back against the wall.

"Father, thank You for Your help today. Thank You that You kept me from crashing on the beach. Thank You also for the storm. Thank You for its beauty and the time I have to spend with You. Help me, Father, to get these girls out of here and back to their families, and give me patience in dealing with them. In Jesus' name. Amen."

Josh sat and listened to the rain and wind. Suddenly, the door of the airplane came open and the wind and rain came inside along with Megan and Sarah. Josh jumped to his feet and went to help them with the door.

"This storm is really something!" said Sarah.

"Yeah, it is," he said.

"I'll get right to the point. Megan said that you told her about Jesus. Is that right?" said Sarah.

Josh just nodded. He really didn't know what to say. *Here she goes*, he thought. *I've got another Shelly on my hands.* Josh waited for her to go on.

"Josh, I'm a Christian, too. A silent Christian and I don't like it. I want to be the one to tell people about Jesus like you did. I want to be someone that can tell people how much God loves them like you did," Sarah blurted out with tears running down her face.

The whole thing embarrassed Josh. He didn't know what to say. It wasn't too long ago that he was just like Sarah. Josh reached out and put his hand on Sarah's arm. Megan put one hand on Josh's arm and the other on Sarah's.

"Father, give Sarah boldness. Give all of us boldness and courage. Help us never to be ashamed of the gospel again. In Jesus' name. Amen."

CHAPTER 10

When Doug Powers and Bill MacIntosh walked into the cabin, Josh's mom was on her knees by their bed. Her eyes were red from crying.

"Honey, what's wrong? Where is Joshua and the Goose?" asked Doug.

"Joshua didn't come home last night. I told him he could take the Goose over to Camp Wildwood yesterday. I thought he would be back before dark, but he didn't come."

"There was a bad storm yesterday afternoon. Nobody could fly. He's probably all right," said Doug.

"Where is this Camp Wildwood?" Bill asked.

"I don't know exactly. Who is this girl on the bed?" said Doug. "Is she the one you went up in the mountains to get?"

"This is Shelly. She is one of the girls from the camp. After we got to Megan, Josh flew her over to the camp. She stayed and Josh brought back Shelly," said Liz.

[124]

"Shelly?" Doug said as he walked over next to the bed. "Shelly, would you go with us and show us where Camp Wildwood is?"

"No, I'm not going because I don't want to. I won't help you. Nobody helped me get to town and a phone," Shelly said, not bothering to turn around.

Puzzled, Doug turned around and looked at Liz. Liz gave him a half-hearted smile and shook her head.

"Doug, we can fly over and take a look around. I'm sure Josh is okay. He probably did the smart thing and waited for the storm to pass," said Bill.

"Do you want to go with us?" said Doug.

"I better stay here with our guest," said Liz. "I can pray from here."

"I'll be fine. I've already been abandoned in this wilderness!" said Shelly. "I don't want to listen to any more praying anyway." Everyone stared at the girl's back and Liz shrugged her shoulders.

"Well, Doug, we have to gas up the Caravan so we don't become a statistic. Liz, that will take us about an hour. We'll have to go over to Hoonah to get it," said Bill. "Then we will go find Josh."

The sun was shining through a window and hit Josh directly in the face as he lay asleep on the floor. He tried to turn over so his back was to the sun, but it only reflected off the shiny aluminum wall. Josh stood up and stretched, then sat down on one of the seats.

Megan and Sarah had stayed until after midnight, then went back to their cabin in the rain. It had been a night of encouragement and talking about what the Lord had done for them. But now the day was clear and bright, and they had to get moving. When he got out of the plane and looked across the water, he felt like he could see forever.

Josh went up on the porch of the girl's cabin. There was some noise, so he knocked on the door. There was no response. Josh knocked again.

"What do you want?" came an angry voice from inside.

"Is everybody up? We need to get going to beat the weather," said Josh.

"Go away. We will be ready when we're ready."

Josh decided to try another tactic. "The plane leaves in twenty minutes. If you're not on it, you won't go and I won't be back."

A collective scream came from inside the cabin as girls got up and started running around. Josh smiled and walked back to the plane. He pulled both engines through to free them from oil lock and then got inside and went through the checklist. When he got through all he could do, he closed his eyes.

"Father, thank You for our talk last night. It was a big encouragement to me. Help me be a witness for You. Father, You know I need Your help today. Make this a safe trip. Help me with my landing. I don't want it to be like it was yesterday. Give me wisdom and know-how. Help me get these people back to the cabin. In Jesus' name. Amen."

Josh got out of the plane and stood there for a few minutes while Megan and Sarah walked around the back of the plane carrying their small backpacks.

"Is everyone about ready to go?" said Josh.

"Josh, you started a riot in there," laughed Sarah. "They'll be out in a minute."

"Should we pray before we go?" asked Megan, looking down at the ground.

"I think we should," said Sarah. "Megan, do you want to pray for us?"

"I guess so," said Megan. All three of them locked arms and bowed their heads.

"God, I've only done this two times in my life. Thank You that Josh came back to rescue me. Thank You he came here to pick us up. Help him fly today. Please keep us safe. Thank You, God. Amen."

Sarah reached over and hugged Megan. Almost all the girls were standing and watching what went on. The two girls dressed like they were going to the beach started to hug each other and say mocking things.

"If everyone is here, get in the plane and buckle up. Throw your backpacks and suitcases in the back of the plane," Josh said, trying to get the attention off the beach girls.

"The nerd, Brenda, isn't here yet," said one of the beach girls. Josh looked around and counted the girls. He realized the girl who was dressed up with the fake mink stole was not there.

"Everybody get in the plane. I'll start the engines. That should bring her," said Josh. "Sarah, would you stand here by the door and wait for Brenda?"

Sarah nodded and threw her backpack into the plane. She helped all the girls with their suitcases and backpacks.

"Megan, would you ride in the co-pilot's seat? I need someone friendly up there with me," said Josh.

"Oh, I would love to! I want to see how to fly this plane," said Megan as she crawled through the door and made her way to the front.

"Excuse me," Josh said as he stepped in front of one of the girls and got into the airplane behind Megan. He threaded his way between the seats and the girls as he went to the cockpit. Sitting down in the pilot's seat, he took the checklist and handed it to Megan.

"You need to slide your seat forward and buckle your seatbelt. I'm down to where it says to prime the engines. When I tell you, read off each item that is left," said Josh.

[128]

Megan slid her seat forward, buckled herself in, then picked up the list and started to read through it. When Josh was ready he looked over at Megan.

"Okay, I'm ready," he said.

"Prime number one engine."

Josh repeated everything she said, reached up and unlatched the primer, pulled it out and pushed it in three times, and then looked back at Megan.

"Advance throttle." Josh pushed the throttle lever forward.

"Turn master switch on." She watched him as he turned it on.

"Start the engine," she said.

Josh pushed the starter button and the engine turned over slowly. He advanced the throttle a little farther and the engine started. The airplane shook as the engine roared to life. They sat there with the engine running for five minutes. Josh thought the noise would bring the last girl, but it didn't seem to help.

"I think we should go and leave her here," came a voice from the back of the plane.

Josh looked over at Megan and smiled. Megan just rolled her eyes.

"I think I better shut down the engine. She's taking a long time. Maybe someone can go get her," he said.

"It won't help. She is the slowest thing ever," said Megan. Josh reached up and shut down the engine. The silence was a relief.

"I'm going to get her," said Sarah. "I think I can get her to come before we leave her out here alone."

Josh nodded as Sarah moved to the back of the plane and crawled out through the door. Megan sighed, closed her eyes, and leaned back in the seat.

"That girl," she said.

They sat there for what seemed like an hour. Josh was eager to get going, but the weather seemed to be holding. The sky was beautiful, blue, and clear. The sun was glistening on the water. It was a great day for flying. He just wished they could get going.

Josh got up and walked to the back of the plane. The girls were all sitting asleep or staring out of the window. He crawled through the door and stood outside the plane looking up toward the cabins.

"Where is that girl?" he said under his breath.

Sarah walked out of the cabin and turned around. "Come on, Brenda. We're going to leave you," she said.

"I have to pack!" the girl yelled.

"Do you want to get out of here or not?" said Sarah. "Have your mother buy you new clothes!"

Sarah turned and started toward the plane. She got halfway back when Brenda came hobbling out of the cabin. Her high heels were twisting and turning as she tried to walk across the loose ground.

"Wait for me, Sarah. Please!" Brenda shouted.

Sarah turned back around and put one of her hands on her hip. When Brenda got up next to her, Sarah took her arm and helped her walk to the plane.

"Glad you could join us," Josh said when they got up next to the plane. He crawled back through the door and walked up to the front.

When Brenda got into the plane she acted like nothing was wrong.

"Hi, everybody. They rushed me. My mother and I are going to have to buy all new clothes. What a disappointment," said Brenda.

One of the beach girls sat up and took off her sunglasses. "Oh, please!" she said and leaned back into her seat, slipping her glasses back on.

Josh shook his head and Megan said, "That girl!" Josh got up and walked back to the door. He reached out, closed it, and made sure it was latched.

"Everybody, buckle your seatbelts. It might be a rough ride at first. Keep them buckled all the time. And stay in your seats." He walked slowly to the front of the plane, checking to make sure they all followed his instructions.

"Oh, Mr. Pilot. I can't find my seatbelt. Could you be a dear and help me, please?" said Brenda.

Josh walked back to Brenda in the last seat, reached down, pulled the seatbelt up, and handed it to her.

"Thank you," she said and winked at Josh. "You are so kind."

"Brenda! You're a jerk!" snapped the same beach girl.

Josh walked back to the front and sat down. They continued through the checklist and started both engines.

"Well, here it goes," he said as he pushed the throttle up, released the parking brake, and started the plane rolling toward the water. When it got to the edge of the water, Josh slowed down and rolled in gently. He taxied out until he felt the airplane start to float.

"Wheels up," he said, pointing at the lever. Megan reached up and moved the lever up. The green light came on. Josh put the flaps down twenty degrees, then turned the plane up the bay. He wanted to make sure he didn't go out into the open ocean. When he got to the back of the channel, he turned the plane around and pointed it toward the ocean.

"Everybody, ready!" Josh yelled to the back of the plane. Nobody responded.

Sarah looked around. "It looks like we're ready."

Josh slowly pushed the power in and the airplane started to wallow in the water. Soon it gained speed, smoothed out, then got up on the step. The airplane raced smoothly along the water and then lifted into the air. Josh held the controls steady and let the plane climb slowly into the sky. When they got out over the ocean, Josh sighed in relief.

Slowly, Josh started a climbing turn to the left and got up higher than the mountains. When he came to a heading of ninety degrees, he started to fly straight across the island.

The weather was holding so Josh started to relax. It was a beautiful day for flying. The two or three clouds that had formed were small. He better keep an eye on them to see if they were going to build. His eyes moved around to every instrument on the panel to see if everything was going as it should. When he was satisfied, he leaned back in his seat and looked out the window.

"Father, thank You for Your great love that protected us on the takeoff. Help us—" Josh's prayer was cut short. Coming out of the cowling on the left engine up above his head was a stream of dark liquid. He didn't know if it was oil or gasoline. As he watched, the stream stopped. Josh wondered if he should shut the engine down. He decided he could wait.

The waiting lasted about three seconds. Black, billowing smoke came pouring out of the cowling and the engine started to run rough. That scared Josh. He reached up to the throttle for the left engine and pulled it to the off position. Then his hand flew over to the switch and shut the left engine down. With that done, he reached for the prop lever and feathered the propeller. The engine slowed down and came to a stop.

"What happened, Josh?" said Megan.

"We lost an engine. It should fly on the other one though," Josh said, trying to sound braver than he felt. There were loud screams coming from the back of the plane as Sarah stuck her head into the cockpit.

"What's going on, Josh? The engine just quit," said Sarah. "Everyone is in a panic in the back."

"Tell them the airplane will fly on one engine and for all of them to buckle their seatbelts and pray," said Josh. "Megan, maybe you better go back and help Sarah get the girls calmed down." Megan nodded, got out of her seat, and went to the back of the airplane.

Josh heard Sarah yell, "Be quiet and listen! Don't panic. Josh says the airplane can fly on one engine. We all need to pray!"

The plane was losing altitude. He hadn't done anything to the engine that was still running, but the airplane was going down slowly. They had lost about three hundred feet and the mountains were getting dangerously close.

He pushed the throttle forward on the running engine. He watched the temperature gauge as it started to climb. Josh knew this engine wouldn't last if the temperature got too high. The engine would slowly start to destroy itself, but he didn't know what else to do.

"Father, You know our situation. You know the one engine is all we have left. Please make this engine last until we can get over the ridge and back to the cabin. Protect these people. Let me get them back to the cabin. In Jesus' name. Amen."

CHAPTER 11

Josh watched as the altitude kept slipping. The part that scared him were the trees on top of the mountain. He thought he could clear them, but only by one hundred feet. The temperature on the engine was still rising. It was starting to get extremely hot. The engine was starting to trail a small amount of smoke. Josh turned his head toward the back of the plane and yelled.

"Megan, I need your help!"

Megan came to the front of the plane, sat down, and buckled her seatbelt. She looked out at the left engine that had stopped, turned, then looked out at the right engine. She gasped when she saw it too was trailing smoke.

"Megan, do you see any flames or anything?"

"No, I only see a little smoke coming out of the bottom of the engine," she said.

"The trees are getting close. I hope we make it over the ridge," he said.

Josh reached up and gave it a little more power. The trailing smoke got worse. He had to make it over the top. Megan had closed her eyes and folded her hands. Her lips were moving in a silent prayer.

When they crossed the top of the ridge the trees were reaching up a few feet below the bottom of the airplane. Josh pulled back on the throttle of the remaining engine and slowed it down.

"That was close," he said. Megan opened her eyes and looked out the window.

"It was really close. God got us through it though," said Megan.

"The airplane is going to lose altitude because I had to slow the engine down. The mountains drop away here so we should be okay."

Megan closed her eyes again and started to pray. Josh adjusted the trim and put the flaps down ten degrees to give it a little more lift. From this point on he knew he had about twenty minutes to the cabin. If the plane would just hold on.

Josh looked out the front window and saw the speck of another airplane coming toward him. It was good to see someone else, but he knew it wouldn't do any good up in the air. He tried to radio his dad, but no one answered. There might be a mountain in the way or maybe his dad wasn't back yet. He thought he would try.

He figured if he got up close to the other airplane they would see his one engine was out and the other engine was smoking. They would know he was in trouble and might have to ditch the airplane. But what could they do?

As the airplane got closer, Josh saw the Cessna Caravan on floats. The plane looked familiar, but he was busy flying. He kept glancing at the plane and noticed it had come up to his altitude. When they passed their closing speed was so fast he couldn't see the pilot.

"Joshua, it's your dad," came the familiar voice over the radio.

"Dad, where are you?"

"I'm in the Caravan that just passed you. We are circling around and will pull up on your right side."

Josh waited for what seemed like an hour for the plane to come up next to him. He was losing altitude and hoped he could at least make it to the water. The one running engine was slowing down and smoke was billowing out behind.

"Joshua, you have about five more minutes until you're over water. If you need to land that would be the best place. Did you pick up the girls?"

"Dad, I have all the girls here."

"If the engine stops you need to maintain about one hundred miles per hour. You'll lose altitude fast."

The engine on the plane backfired and slowly stopped. Josh reached up and pumped the throttle, but it didn't do anything. He grabbed the wheel with both hands and tried to hold the plane up, but all it did was slow down to a dangerous speed. The silence startled everyone and a loud scream came from the back of the airplane.

"Joshua," said his dad in a calm voice. "You can do this, Son. Just listen to me. Don't pull back on the wheel. Let the airplane start down. Put the flaps all the way down. Remember, let it fly about a hundred miles per hour."

Josh released the back pressure on the wheel and the nose of the plane started down steeper than he liked. They were a few miles from the coast and the trees were coming up fast. He put the flaps down all the way. That seemed to slow the airplane but he had to drop the nose to maintain one hundred miles per hour. That made the distance to water seem impossible.

Josh glanced over at Megan. "Tell everyone to make sure their seatbelts are pulled real tight, and then get back here."

Megan nodded, got up, and crawled into the back of the plane. He could hear her talking but didn't know what was being said.

"Father, You know the situation. You know how this scares me. Whatever the outcome, please save us. Give me wisdom on what to do. Keep me calm. Protect us now."

The trees at the edge of the water looked like they were taller and reached up in the sky higher than they were. He tried to point the airplane between them. He hoped that they were far enough apart for the wings to pass through.

"Dad, the trees look like they're too tall. I think we're going to hit them!"

"Son, maintain your glide slope. Maintain your airspeed. You'll be all right."

"Megan, sit down and get buckled up!" Josh yelled into the back.

Megan came up and crawled back into the seat, buckled her seatbelt, looked out at the trees, and immediately started to pray. The trees were only a few feet below the bottom of the plane.

Josh heard the scraping sounds of Sitka spruce on the hull of the airplane and pulled back on the wheel. The plane slowed and climbed a few feet. When the stall warning horn sounded, Josh dropped the nose and started down for the next tree. He repeated this process several times before he ran out of sky.

There was one last tree before he got to the water. On both sides of the plane were two giant spruce trees that he couldn't get over. He would have to fly between them. He didn't know if he could clear the tree in the middle. He turned off both fuel selectors and the master switch. To be this close to water and crash into a tree seemed too much.

Josh waited to the last second and then pulled back on the control wheel. The airplane slowed again and climbed, but it was not high enough. Each wing scraped through the spruce. The lower tree in the center slammed into the hull, breaking off four feet of the top. Josh hoped it was all that happened.

He couldn't think about that anymore. He had to land the airplane and he was down to less than a hundred feet from the water. Everything was going fast.

"Hold that altitude, Son. You're doing fine."

Josh knew his dad didn't want to make a big deal out of the tree. Not now, anyway. Josh could see the Caravan out of the corner of his eye. He didn't want to look at it because something might happen when he looked away.

He glanced at his airspeed just when the stall warning horn sounded. He was still thirty feet out of the water, so he dropped the nose again. When he got down just above the water he pulled back on the wheel and started to slow the plane. It settled onto the water in a perfect landing. Without any power the plane slowed quickly and stopped.

All the girls in the back of the plane started to applaud. Megan reached over, put her hand on Josh's arm, and said, "Thank the Lord!"

"Amen," was all Josh could say.

Josh watched the Caravan land and taxi back to them. The Goose was a long way from shore and had no power.

Josh got out of his seat, crawled under the dashboard to the nose of the plane, and opened the hatch. He saw the water seeping in next to a spar on the bottom of the plane. When he stood up through the hatch, his dad was standing on the float of the Caravan.

"That was a great landing," said his dad.

"Dad, the water is coming in the bottom of the plane. We have to get it to shore."

His dad threw one end of a rope to Josh. It fell short. His dad pulled the rope back and threw it again. The same thing happened. Josh started to crawl out of the hatch but Megan stopped him.

"Josh, let me go. I was a lifeguard and I can swim in cold water. You need to stay dry." Megan pushed her way up in the front of the hatch.

"Mr. Powers, leave the rope. I'll get it." Before his dad could say anything, Megan dove into the water. She swam out to the rope, picked it up, swam back to Josh, and threw the rope up to him.

"This water is freezing."

"I would have gone," said Josh.

"I know you would, but I wanted to do something." Megan turned around, swam to the Caravan, and pulled herself up onto the float.

"I'm going to tie this to one of the struts," said his dad. "We will have to take it easy when we pull you in."

Josh waved and tied the rope to the cleat on the front of the seaplane, then waved again. He watched his dad turn and say something to the other pilot. Mac started the engine on the Caravan and turned it toward shore. When the rope was tight he revved the engine until the Goose started to move. Josh ducked back inside and took his seat. The two planes moved slowly across the water until the Caravan was almost to the shore. Mac increased the speed and then turned off to the right.

Josh turned on the master switch and lowered the landing gear. The Goose slowed and then the wheels hit the ground. Josh crawled back to the hatch at the front of the plane. He looked at the dry ground twenty feet ahead. The tire on the plane had raised the nose up out of the water.

When the Caravan was parked beside him, Josh said, "Dad, do you think that all of us could pull the plane up on the beach?"

"We can try," said his dad.

"The beach looks steep," said Mac. "That airplane is heavy, but I think it will come up some because the tail is still floating."

"We have to get it out of the water because it is leaking. There are a couple of inches of water inside right now," said Josh.

"God had His hand on the plane when you struck the tree," said his dad.

Josh ducked back down into the hatch and went to the back. All the girls started to talk at the same time.

"People! People, we have to get off the plane," Josh shouted. He was drowned out by a loud moan. "We can't go out the door because the water is too deep. You'll have to go up to the nose and go through the hatch. It's only about fifteen feet to the beach."

The two beach girls jumped to their feet. "We're ready," they said in unison.

"Go up through the cockpit and crawl under the instrument panel to the nose of the plane. The hatch is already open. Go out on the nose and let yourself down to the ground."

The other girls were starting to line up when Josh heard one of them yell, "I don't want to do this!" Josh went to the hatch and stuck his head out. One of the girls was standing on the shore, the other was hanging off the side of the plane with a firm grasp of the side of the opening. Her legs were pulled up under her.

When she saw Josh she said, "The water is freezing! I don't want to get wet!"

"Let go, Kim. The water is not that cold," said Megan.

"No! I don't want to," said the girl.

Megan waded out into the water and started to tickle the girl. She thrashed around, slipped, and fell into the water.

She came up sputtering and soaked. When she stood up she noticed the water didn't even come up to her shorts.

"Megan! Why did you do that?" the girl shouted as she walked up on the beach and stood by her friend.

Megan just laughed as Josh ducked back into the airplane so the girl wouldn't see him laughing.

"Okay girls, let's get going," he said with a big smile on his face. All the others got in line and jumped off the plane without saying a word.

Josh was surprised when he saw Brenda sitting in one of the seats trying to look like a princess.

"Brenda, get going. We have to push this airplane up on the beach."

"Mr. Pilot, can you carry me to the shore so I won't get wet and dirty?" said Brenda.

"With those high heels you'll only get your legs wet. Get going."

"Humph!" she said as she got up and staggered to the front of the plane.

Josh sat down in the pilot's seat and picked up a little piece of rope they had used for a control lock. He pulled back on the wheel and tied it. He started to get up when he heard a loud scream. Josh jumped out of the seat and crawled to the hatch. He slid off the front of the airplane into two feet of water.

Brenda was thrashing around in the water like she was drowning. He reached down, took her hand, and pulled her to her feet. Two more steps and down she went again. When she fell the second time, all the girls started to laugh. Josh heard one of them say, "What a nerd!"

"You need to take off your high heels so you can get out of the water," he said.

"You'd like that, wouldn't you?" snapped the girl.

"I want you to stand up and walk out of the water and the only way you can do it is if you take off your shoes," he said.

"Fine!" she sputtered.

Josh waited for her to take off her shoes and offered his hand. This time, she refused it. Josh pulled his hand back and shrugged.

"I'm going to tell my mother and she is going to be mad!" shouted Brenda as she stomped out of the water and stood by the other girls.

"Joshua, it looks like it's high tide or close to it. We have to get this plane up a little farther out of the water. Mac and I will wade out into the deep water and push the tail. Get one or two of the girls to push one of the landing gear and you push the other side. Have the rest of the girls pull on the rope," said his dad.

"Dad, I don't think—" Josh stopped before he said something unkind.

"I'll go out and push on the landing gear," said Megan.

"The rest of you girls get on the rope and pull it when I tell you," said Josh.

"Come on, girls. Let's show these guys how strong we are," said Sarah as she picked up the rope.

All the girls mumbled and picked up the rope, except for Brenda. "I am not going to pull on that rope!" she said as she turned her back and walked away.

The two men waded out into the water by the tail of the plane. The water only came up to their waist. The airplane was sitting on flat ground, but needed to roll up a small rise under the water. Josh and Megan waded out and got behind each landing gear.

"Everybody ready?" said Josh.

"Ready," mumbled a few of the girls half-heartedly.

"On three. One, two, three, push!" Josh yelled.

The plane sat there for a few seconds while everyone strained and then it started to move. It slowly moved up so the front wheels were on the gravel.

"That should do it," said his dad. "We can tie it off so it won't drift away if the wind comes up."

Josh climbed on the airplane and untied the hundred-foot rope. He jumped down, took the end of the rope, and tied it to one of the landing gear struts. The remaining rope he walked around a tree, then back to the other strut, and tied it on.

"You got everything out of the plane?" Josh said to the group of girls. No one spoke up.

"I'll go in and check," said Megan.

Josh and Megan walked up to the front of the plane. Josh cupped his hands and made a stirrup for Megan to get back into the hatch on the nose of the plane.

"Dad, I better go in and see if I shut everything down." His dad came over and gave him a leg up.

When Josh crawled through the hatch, he saw Megan picking up all the jackets and sweatshirts the girls had left behind. She crawled back to the hatch and stood up. Josh watched through the windshield of the plane as she threw them out on the ground.

"Here's all your stuff," said Megan. The girls wandered over to pick up their belongings.

Josh looked at all the instruments and touched all the switches to make sure they were off. He felt bad he had to leave the airplane out in the wilderness, but there was nothing he could do. He also felt bad the airplane engines were both down. He thought it would need a complete overhaul on both engines.

He crawled under the dashboard and up to the hatch. Megan's legs were hanging down through the hole.

"Oh! Sorry, Josh," she said as she moved her legs up out of the hole. Josh stood up as Megan sat looking off into the forest.

"This place is so beautiful," she said. "Look at the trees and waterfalls. Even the animals are beautiful. God's creation is wonderful. And to think, two weeks ago I was so into myself I never noticed. Knowing Jesus does make all things beautiful. I wish all the girls could know Him."

"Why don't you tell them?" Josh said.

"Me? I don't know enough yet."

"Yes, you do. Tell them just like you told me and tell them why."

"I don't know, Josh," she said as she slipped down from the nose of the plane and walked over to the other girls.

Josh got out, closed the hatch, and latched it shut.

"Well, that does it," he said as he jumped off the plane. "We better get going."

CHAPTER 12

Josh and his dad helped the girls get up into the Cessna Caravan.

"Oh. This is a lot nicer than the other airplane," said Brenda as she got into the plane, turned, and glared at Josh. "I bet this pilot knows how to fly."

Josh wanted to say something to her and started to, but his dad stopped him.

"You can't please everyone, Son," said his father as Josh shook his head and started to climb into the back.

"Josh, I want you to ride in the front seat and see how to fly this thing. Maybe Mac will let you fly it on the way back. We got the other airplanes."

Josh nodded, walked up onto the pontoon, and crawled into the right side door. He was glad he didn't have to ride in the back with that girl. He didn't know if he could let her get away with her remarks.

His dad pushed the airplane off the shore and turned it around so it faced down the channel, then he jumped on the pontoon, hoisted himself into the airplane, and shut the door. Josh could hear him as he walked to the front.

"Everyone, buckle your seatbelts, please," he said.

"My dad doesn't make me wear my seatbelt in his airplane," said Brenda.

"That's nice, but this isn't your dad's airplane. On this plane everyone will buckle their seatbelts," said his dad. He came up, stuck his head in the cockpit, and said, "The door is locked and everyone is buckled up."

Mac finished his checklist and started the airplane. It didn't have the throbbing sound of the Goose. It sounded more like a jet.

"This doesn't sound the same as the Goose," said Josh.

"No. This has a PT-6, six-hundred horsepower turbine engine. We can carry twice as many passengers as we have, a full cargo pod underneath, and a tank loaded with gas. This is a nice flying machine. I think you'll learn to like the one your dad got," said Mac.

"I think I will, too," said Josh.

When Mac gave Josh control of the airplane, he was surprised at how easy it was to fly. Josh realized he didn't really know where they were. He looked around at the bay to see if he could spot anything familiar. When he couldn't he said, "Mr. MacIntosh, where are we exactly?"

"We are in Tenakee Strait. You landed the Goose clear up at the north end," said Mac as he pointed to the GPS. "When you get out to the main channel you will need to turn right and fly down to Peril Strait, then fly up that one."

The trip back to the cabin took about half an hour. They had to pick up Shelly and then take the girls to Hoonah so they could call their parents. Josh's mom had already decided to stay in a motel with the girls until they could be picked up.

When Josh had the cabin in sight, Mac said, "You better let me have it from here. Keep your hands on the wheel and follow me through the landing."

Josh nodded as Mac reached up and took the wheel. He liked this airplane and he knew he would like to fly it again someday. He watched as Mac made a straight in landing. He would have to circle the cabin and land going away from it, but Mac knew right where to land and how much distance it would take to stop in the water. Josh would know that too someday.

When the pontoons were up far enough on the wooden dock and the engine had come to a stop, Josh opened his door and climbed down. He turned toward the passenger door and saw his dad was already letting the girls out onto the pontoon. Josh turned back around and jumped off the pontoon down onto the dock. His mother was standing there.

"Where's the Goose, Joshua?" said his mom.

"We had to leave it in Tenakee Strait. Both engines died," said Josh.

"And he did a great job landing the plane," said Megan as she walked up. "I thought it was the best one he has ever made, but it was only the second one I made with him. We're all safe here now."

His dad walked over to the group and handed Josh a cell phone with a large black antenna sticking out of the side.

"Joshua, this is a satellite phone I borrowed from Mac. I want you to call Ron Gilbert and tell him what happened to the Goose and where it is," said his dad.

"Dad, can't you call him for me? I'm too embarrassed to call. Please?" said Josh.

"Joshua, you decided to take the airplane and you did a great thing rescuing all the girls, but you were the one flying the plane. You have the responsibility to tell Ron what happened to it."

"Dad, please, I don't want to."

"Father, give my son the courage and boldness to make this phone call. Please give Ron understanding and let Joshua find favor with him. In Your Son's name. Amen," prayed his dad.

Josh took the phone from his dad. His heart felt heavy, but he knew his father was right. He had decided to fly the Goose over to get the girls and it was his responsibility to make the call.

"I dialed Ron's number in so when you are ready all you have to do is send it," said his dad.

Josh walked up on the porch of the cabin. He was nervous and paced back and forth. When he finally pressed the button on the phone, he closed his eyes and prayed, "Lord, help me make this call." Josh hoped no one would answer. It took a long time for the call to go through. The phone rang once and a woman's voice was on the other end.

"Hello, Gilbert's Flying Service. How can I help you?"

"Ah…this is Josh…Joshua Powers, Doug Powers' son. Can I speak with Ron Gilbert, please?"

"One moment, please."

Josh felt like he waited an eternity.

"Hi, this is Ron. What can I do for you?"

"Mr. Gilbert, this is Josh Powers, Doug—" was all he got out of his mouth.

"Joshua Powers. I know who you are. Saw you in the jungle when you were a little squirt. I haven't seen you in ten years. How're you doing, Son?"

"I am not doing so good. I need to talk to you about the Grumman Goose you loaned my dad." Josh tried to stall before he told him.

"Did the right engine quit on you? It was out of time. Needs an overhaul."

"Mr. Gilbert, I had to fly over to the other side of the island to pick up seven stranded girls and on the way back the right engine quit. I worked the left engine too hard and it quit, too." There, he got it out. Now he just had to wait for the consequences.

"Everyone okay? I hope you were over the water when it quit."

"We were. The plane hit a tree and there is a little damage to the hull—it leaks a little. The dead stick landing went okay, but your airplane is on the north end of Tenakee Strait. It is tied to a tree."

"It always leaked. Glad you're okay," said Ron. "My son, Jason, is fishing down in those parts. I'll have him tow the airplane back here."

"I'm sorry, Mr. Gilbert," Josh said.

"No apology is necessary, Joshua. I knew that engine was going to go sometime. Don't even worry about it. I got a couple of A&P mechanics that owe me. I'll have them overhaul it. Don't even worry about it."

"Thank you, Mr. Gilbert. Thank you very much."

"Think nothing of it. Give my regards to your parents."

"Thank you again, Mr. Gilbert. I will." Josh pushed the button on the phone to end the call and sighed in relief.

He walked back to his parents with a big smile on his face. He handed the phone back to his dad.

"Did you call him?" asked his dad.

"Yeah, he said not to worry about it."

"Joshua, Ron told me the engine was going to fail and not to worry about it. Just be over the water when it does. You did a great job getting the airplane down. I wanted you to call him because you were flying it."

"We better get these girls back to Hoonah," said Mac.

"And I have an airplane to pick up," said his dad.

All the girls started to move over to the Caravan and get in. Josh's mom went up to the cabin and stuck her head in the door. A minute later, Shelly came out of the cabin and walked ten feet behind Liz.

"Dad, I don't think I am going to go over to Hoonah. I'm going to stay here," said Josh.

"We may not be back tonight," said his dad.

"That's all right. I want to rest and spend time with the Lord."

Megan walked up to Josh and kissed him on the cheek. "Thank you so much for all you have done for me. Thank you for introducing me to Jesus. I'll never forget you," she said. Josh looked at the ground, embarrassed. She jogged over to the airplane, climbed in, then turned and waved.

Josh watched as the plane taxied out for takeoff, accelerated, then lifted into the air.

"Thank You, Father, that I was able to bring those girls back safely. Thank You that Mr. Gilbert was understanding. Thank You for Your love, for saving Megan, and awakening Sarah," Josh prayed.

73113110R00087

Made in the USA
Columbia, SC
02 September 2019